Leahcim a

By

Registration number TXu 2-072-582
THIS IS A WORK OF FICTION. CHARACTERS, NAMES, PLACES AND
EVENTS ARE A PRODUCT OF THE AUTHORS IMAGINATION.

COVER DESIGN BY KATHY FULTON

KFULT8@AOL.COM

ACKNOWLEGEMENTS

God the Father, God the Son, God the Holy Spirit. Thank you for the inspiration, courage, and talent (on loan) to write this book. I pray that it is a blessing to your children. Amen

Dedication

I was 13 years old when I met the women who would become my wife. I remember asking God, begging him, if I could please marry her one day. Seventeen years later my prayer was answered.

Now this week, on our 27th wedding anniversary, she is reading the first ninety pages of this book. For over 27 years she has tolerated all of my hair brained ideas and the failures that they became. She stuck with me through all of them. And as I look back, I realize that out of all the life experiences that I have had...the failures, the disappointments, the successes that life can bring... I have only one regret. That is the times that I have squandered the greatest blessing that God has given me... my wife and her love. There is no greater gift to me, no greater blessing than her.

If you're reading this book it will be because she, my wife, has once again been asked to follow one more dream with me. It is her opinion, and hers alone, that will decide in my mind whether or not I finish this endeavor. You see, God said, "and the two shall become one." And of course, my daughter Lyndsey, who at the age of 24 has gone from being the student to the teacher. It's amazing how that happens. I'm not even sure when it happened. But in her young life she has taught me to become patient and loving to so many things, that in my ignorance I would have not tolerated.

It goes without saying, these two are the loves of my life.

FOR GABRIELLE (STARR)
You were the inspiration for this story.
That little light that shines so bright in you, I can't wait until you let it grow!
Love you.

FORWARD

I was about 11 or 12 years old the first time I heard the voice of God.

I was living with my father on a small farm in Colorado. He was an abusive man, not a drinker just an angry man. His anger always spilled out onto my brother and I. It came in the form of beatings, and for an 11-year-old, this is confusing to say the least.

I always believed there was a God. I'm not sure where that came from, my grandmother most likely, but I knew he was there.

My grandmother's house was on the same farm as ours and was a sanctuary for my brother and I when we needed to hide from my father. I remember standing outside her house one night... I was hiding after a beating, crying out to God, "Why don't you just take me and end this!?"

I looked at our garage across the way. It had no doors, just four walls and a roof. If it had doors, I would have gone in and started the car and just end it myself, I had thought. And that's when I heard His quiet, soft voice that said "Because I have great plans for your life."

I can't explain in words the effect this had on me at that moment, but it was enough, it brought peace to my soul. I went on with my life that night, and I've held that voice, and those words, in my heart ever since.

It would be 28 years before I found out his name.

Emerson wrote a fantastic line in one of his books he said...

"There is something I do not know, the knowing of which would change everything."

I spent 28 years looking for the 'something'. When I read those words from Emerson it resonated in my soul. Yes, there's a something and it has a name I know it does! And so I prayed, that whoever 'he' was, that I needed to know the real Him, and to please show me who he really is. In August of 2001, I became a believer.

After 39 years of doing life my way, drugs, alcohol, lust, etc. ...and searching religions from A to Z... God in his grace and in *His* way, brought me to the end of myself, and revealed His true self to me.

Now, something other believers did not tell me, was that when you first believe sometimes it can be like painting a big bullseye on your back. What I mean is this, Lucifer does not like this, and sometimes as was the case with me, he tries to get you to change your mind. My daughter was about 8 years old when I first believed, in fact we were baptized on the same day.

She was having trouble sleeping in her room due to "something evil" in there. So, she slept in our room in the 'Big bed'. I began having weird dreams, the first and most memorable, I was climbing a spiral stair case in what was a brick tower. I vividly remember, I was running up this stairwell, all the walls around me were made of bricks. As I reached the top, a man was standing there leaning against the wall. I remember he had long, brown shoulder length hair, and he had one knee up against the wall, his arms crossed with his back to me.

As I reached the top he said, "Are you ready to fight?" As he turned to face me I saw he had a sword in his hand, and I was terrified.

My response was "I don't have a sword."

He replied, "Too bad, I do," and he began to chase me down the staircase.

As I reached the bottom there was a locked iron gate, and I couldn't get through! He was coming upon me fast! I looked around and there, in the wall, was a grey colored brick. All the others were red and brown typical colored bricks, this one was different! I pushed on the brick and a mighty wind came out of the locked gate, hitting the man and stopping his pursuit. When the wind hit him he said, "Don't try your father's tricks on me!"

Hmmm, interesting, right? So, I asked my mentor, a wonderful woman named Ruth, who was guiding me through this new found walk with God. She said it was Lucifer – only she called him Satan (an overused low impact name today) – and that I shouldn't be surprised if he returned to finish the fight. She said when he returns you get out of bed and stand up and say 'GOD IS MY DEFENDER I WILL NOT BE MOVED!' She said to repeat this for as long as it takes, and he will leave. She explained that the only defense against Lucifer's attacks was the word of God (that was my sword) and that being a new believer I really needed to start studying God's word or practicing with my sword.

A few nights later around 2 am he returned. Only this time it wasn't a dream he invaded he actually woke me up! I was sleeping soundly, and I remember feeling like someone was standing next to my bed, you know that feeling. As I opened my eyes, I saw in the dark something darker than the dark itself. He had no definition to his features just this darkness in the form of a body. Just as I realized that there was something in the room, he flew across my chest. I felt the wind from his movement go over me, and to my horror, he slammed into my daughter causing her to physically jump. She didn't wake up, her body just kind of jumped at the impact. He slid off her and by now I was on my feet. I didn't see where he went, but I started saying what Ruth had taught me "GOD IS MY DEFENDER, I WILL NOT BE MOVED!" I said it over and over as I moved from room to room throughout the entire house.

The next day I was at Ruth's house first thing in the morning. She explained that he really was nothing to fear, and that he was just testing the water so to speak. She said that I was now sealed in the Holy Spirit, and that Lucifer could not take my salvation. But he would most likely spend the rest of my life 'messing with me', trying to get me to stumble. She told me he may return, and just to be sure that I had a sword. (The God is my defender scripture.)

He did return one more time, in a dream that night. I was standing in a dry place like a desert. A few sparse trees were scattered around, and there he was, the man from the stairwell again.

"Are you ready?" he asked as he drew his sword. He moved toward me, his sword raised.

I was swinging my sword hitting his. I remember the sound of the steel hitting steel as we fought. I kept repeating the words as I swung. I turned and swung, hitting him in the mid torso area as I screamed "GOD IS MY DEFENDER!" When I stuck him, he turned to dust and fell into a pile of ash on the ground.

The next thing I recall, was God and I walking in heaven (I assume), I only saw his back. He was wearing a white robe and I was walking next to him. He put his arm around my shoulder as we walked, and he said, "Good job," as I recounted the whole battle scene with him.

The next day I was back at Ruth's, and she gave me a bottle of anointing oil. She told me to walk the entire house and "seal" every window, door, fireplace and any openings that demons or Satan might come through.

I did, and to my amazement, that night my daughter slept in her room saying, "It was ok now."

As the next 16 years have rolled by, I have studied God's word. Lucifer has left me alone for the most part. There's always the constant attempt to sway my judgment. He has put traps all around me, and I have stepped into quite a few! But, he has never come back to my house, or my dreams that I recall.

I have often thought of those early battles, and I have always wanted to document them. So, there you have it. Those stories are true. The one you're about to read is not, but... it could be...enjoy.

LEAHCIM
AN UNORTHADOX ANGEL
BOOK ONE
BY TED FULTON

Prelude

Leahcim was pacing back and forth chewing his fingernail saying, "Oh dear, oh dear, oh dear, oh my, oh my, oh my! What've I done! What have I done!"

Pacing and looking at the bodies, chewing his fingernail back and forth. Pacing looking, pacing looking.

"Oh my, oh my... please get up, please get up." He said.

He thought, *if they get up then they're okay and everything will be fine. If their spirits get up, but their bodies stay on the ground then.... oh, my, oh my... oh this is terrible! My first assignment by myself. I blew it! I blew it*, he thought. *First, I missed the staircase, no one has ever done that! Then I missed the interaction! No one has ever done that either. I fell from the sky... absolutely terrifying! That's never happened either... not to any angel in the history of angels... oh my, oh my... and now my subjects are dead! They weren't supposed to die! There was nothing in the file about them dying! Oh man I'm in big trouble...*

He looked at the bodies again "PLEASE GET UP!" he screamed.

CHAPTER 1
The Fall

Leahcim, (pronounced Leah-kim), as angels go was a rather large, slightly chubby fellow.
He was a little clumsy, somewhat aloof, and easily distracted. But nonetheless committed to his task. He spoke with an English accent. He wasn't English, but he had spent 87 years in England with a subject early in his training, and the accent just kind of stuck.

Leahcim was headed down the staircase that angels use to go back and forth from heaven. Normally on their way to or from an assignment with their subjects, humans. Well, it's not a staircase anymore, they changed it to an escalator in the early seventies.

There was a trial in heaven today. Which meant that all angels had to be on the staircase headed back from their assignments no later than the 3rd bell. Heaven used these occasions to send angels in training to their first assignments, all by themselves. It was a good occasion to give these trainees their first hands-on alone experience. Think of it as a practical exam. The last phase of three hundred years of training, and these were always planned around 'slow news days', if you will.

Leahcim was an angel in training. He had been training for three hundred years and he was approaching his final year. Today was a very big day. Today he was going to speak all by himself, with no trainer nearby. Today, Leahcim, for a very short period gets to be a guardian angel. In actuality, the time span will be approximately two minutes. The instructions for his interaction given to him by his trainer for this was brief,

"Backseat, whisper left lane."

And that was it.

Leahcim's trainer was a very old angel. In fact, so old that he was there to witness the messenger deliver the greatest message of all time, the Virgin Birth! Leahcim would listen for hours as his trainer told stories of old. For years Leahcim watched his trainer as he would speak, whisper thoughts, ideas, and suggestions into the ears of their subjects. Sometimes they would actually hear and heed the suggestion, warning or thought. Other times, they would just ignore it and well... calamity.

It's important to note that guardian angels also have the ability to muse animals. Animals are very easy, you simply tell them what to do and they do it. (i.e., God making a donkey talk)

He'd been practicing for weeks the two words that he was given to speak. He would stand in front of the mirror and practice. Sometimes in a forceful voice, sometimes in a loud scream other times in a soft whisper, sometimes with an accent sometimes without. He just couldn't decide. He'd been trying to figure out what these words meant and why he had to speak them. They didn't make sense, the two words. Left lane... what could it mean?

He had always hoped that the first time he got to speak it would be something grand like "Take your sword and fight!"... or a virgin birth...well that one had already been done. But nevertheless, these words *must* be important because they only speak when it's of the utmost importance!

He had decided on a whisper, close but not too close. Sometimes, if their ears are open it can be startling, too far away and it might not be heard at all. No, it was decided. In the backseat he would lean forward and whisper "left lane".

He worried to himself "Oh dear, oh dear." Rubbing his hands together, which he always did when he was nervous. Or chewing on his thumb nail while pacing back and forth.

"What if something goes wrong. What if I swallow a fly and can't speak, or what if the radio is too loud and he can't hear me at all! Oh dear."

And then he remembered that speaking isn't the only way that they're able to communicate or nudge. He'd seen his trainer do things like stick out his foot and trip his subject to make them bump into someone they needed to meet. Or hit them in the head with a bucket of fish chum or catch their pants on fire. And once, they even made a cat knock over an oil lamp to catch the house on fire, so that the gallant neighbor would come in and save the day! (Those two ended up getting married.)

Aside from changing free will, there really aren't any lengths that they won't go to, in the pursuit of God's will. And he never forgot what his trainer had told him, when he looked at him with those deep old eyes, and in that very solemn crackly old voice..."Remember my young friend, there is always a backup plan... always."

He'd never seen an occasion for a back-up plan to be used, but he felt much better remembering those words.

As Leahcim stepped onto the escalator his excitement rose, so exciting! He practiced all the way down, "Left lane" he said out loud in a stern voice.

"Left lane please," in a very monotone calm voice.

"*AGGGH LEFT LANE!*" he screamed. The other angels looked at him and giggled. As he reached the bottom he let the angels behind him pass. This was it. He puffed out his chest and got ready to step onto the platform. Suddenly his robe got stuck in the teeth of the escalator. He turned and tugged on it frustrated... then pulled, then yanked, it wouldn't budge.

"First Bell" the voice sounded.

At the third tone of the third bell, the staircase would close, and anyone left on earth would be trapped until it re-opened. (That's never happened.)

Leahcim thought, *There's still time, just two words and back on the escalator.* He pulled harder. He turned and looked at the platform, his eyes were wide, *Ok just pull harder*, he thought. He was straining with all his might, as he turned his body and braced his legs and pulled.

"Second Bell," the voice said.

Now he began to panic.

"What if I miss my interaction!" That had never happened to anyone, missing an interaction could be catastrophic! He pulled harder, now his whole body was leaning with all his weight towards the platform and pulling.

"Third Bell, First Tone" the voice had a slight urgency.

He pulled so hard he was beginning to sweat.

"Third Bell, Second Tone"

Leahcim began to scream "No No No!"

"Third Bell, FINAL Tone." Just then his robe tore loose and Leahcim fell, stumbling across the platform and off the edge... into darkness.

He fell for a really long time, his heart pounding in his chest as he fell. His eyes were wide open and then closed tightly, and he kept falling. He never realized how far it really was from heaven to earth. Then finally he slammed into the ground with a thud and a grunt. He landed on his back staring up at the stars, "Ohhhh...that hurt."

His mind began to race, *What happened? This shouldn't have happened, I should be in the back seat of the car.*

"Oh Lord, I've missed the interaction!" he said. It was more of a confession than a statement.

"Father," he said, "I've missed it, what should I do?" He waited ....no response.

"Father? Hello?"....nothing. Angels speak to God all the time, ask questions and seek guidance all the time. He's always available to them, he's never not there for them. But tonight, there was no answer, it was so quiet he could hear the crickets chirping.

"Hello, can you hear me?...Anyone?" Leahcim's heart sank. For the first time ever, he was alone. He stood up, confused and disoriented, and began to look around. Suddenly he heard a loud roar come up from the other side of a small hill. He saw head lights, then a car came crashing through the trees, over the hill, and went flying through the air, and turned over in midair! It slammed to the ground with a tremendous crash and rolled over two more times. Leahcim could see people falling out of the car as it rolled. It finally came to rest on its tires, headlights still on, and the blinkers flashing through the fog. He could hear the radio playing. He stood there in the silence, stunned at what he had just seen. His heart was pounding as he had a sickening realization...this was the car he was supposed to be in, whispering guidance to the driver.

As he made his way down the hill to the car, he began reasoning with himself.

"Please don't be dead! They can't be dead," he said. "They can't be dead because it wasn't in their file, and if it's not in their file it doesn't happen." He first came upon Johnathan, laying on his back arms spread wide. He wasn't moving and there was blood coming from his head. Leahcim turned and looked for Amy. She was about thirty feet away, face down with her arms at her side.

None of this was supposed to happen! He was supposed to step off the staircase, into the backseat of a car, whisper two words and be back home. Now he wasn't in the backseat of a car, he was in the middle of cow pasture. With two very dead subjects, and a bunch of cows. It was dark, it was cold and foggy, and to top it off he seemed to be in a minefield of cow dung! He was covered in it, his subjects were covered in it, and poor Amy was face down in it!

~ 15 ~

As he stood there in the silence, he could feel the chill in the air. He began pacing and chewing on his thumbnail. Oh he could just hear it now... the only subject to ever be smothered to death by a pile of cow dung! And this would be credited to him, Leahcim – the angel in training! *Great, just great*, he thought.

The car was mangled, his subjects were dead, the staircase was gone. He had no idea what to do next or how to get home. He couldn't even imagine what his trainer was going to say.

As he looked back at Jonathan, there was a stirring...then a groan, and suddenly Jonathan sat straight up! Leahcim's heart jumped but then sank. Jonathan's spirit had sat up, but his body remained on the ground. He *was* dead!

At the same time Amy began to stir. There was a muffled groan and a wriggle, and then she rose to her knees. She coughed and spit, and then swore as she proceeded to fall face first into the very word she had just muttered.

Johnathan had heard her and turned to look. Again, she began to struggle and move, this time she rolled over arms spread out. She coughed and spit again, this time her spit went straight up and right back down on her face.

"Uggggh!" She yelled. "Why is this happening? Oh that smell!"

Leahcim watched in horror as she rolled over and left her body behind, and realized she was dead as well. Johnathan got up, staggered toward her and fell back down. Amy at this point was examining her clothes and hair and gagging at the wretched smell she was covered in.

"My blouse, my Gucci blouse! And my hair," she was crying, -well whining really. Johnathan was on his feet again bent over resting his hands on his knees. Amy clamored to her feet spotting him and began screaming, yet still whining.

"What did you do you idiot!"

"I swerved to miss the bunny," he said.

"It was a rabbit you idiot! And it would have been just as happy being a coat! I have several of them! You could have killed us to save a coat you moron!"

Leahcim chuckled, Amy and Johnathan looked at him startled. And then they screamed! Then Leahcim of course screamed, and they screamed again.

"Who are you?" Johnathan asked. "Did you see what happened?"

"Do you have a mirror?" Amy asked.

Johnathan looked at her and shook his head. Leahcim looked behind him and then back at them. Could they see him? Was there someone behind him? He started walking backwards away from them, chewing his thumb nail as he retreated.

"Come back here!" Amy screamed.

He retreated to a nearby tree and tried to hide behind it, still chewing his thumbnail. *What is going on,* he thought, *they can't possibly see me.* They can never see us, we have only been seen in very rare circumstances! *Oh dear, oh dear, this is bad,* he thought. Johnathan came around the tree, Leahcim screamed "Auggh!"

"Who are you?" Johnathan asked. "Do you have a phone? Have you called for help?"

Amy still engrossed with the cow dung she was covered in, was coming up the hill towards them. Leahcim gathered himself and began to stammer, "I um... I... well, let's see, where to... um...how do I... um, I'm your guardian angel and well... um... you're dead! Sorry, but yes, you're dead. I think. I'm not really sure... but yes... definitely dead... maybe"

"What!?...Dead?" Johnathan said. "I'm standing right here, I'm not dead!"

As Leahcim looked toward Amy, a chill went up his spine. Johnathan, who was seeing the same image, froze. His jaw dropped as he gazed towards Amy.

"What is that?" Johnathan asked.

"Dark ones," Leahcim answered.

Two pale greyish figures were coming up behind Amy. Long arms that nearly touched the ground, with contorted legs. Their faces and heads were hairless with long pointed ears, their cheek bones were very distinct with rotting teeth and drooling mouths. Dark ones were actually demons. Fallen angels, who had been cast out of heaven when Lucifer tried his coup against God. He and a third of the angels of heaven were banished and cast to the earth. Lucifer now had charge of the earth, and all his demons.

When a believer dies, angels are dispatched by God to escort them to heaven. When a non-believer dies the dark ones are dispatched by Lucifer to go gather the soul. On rare occasions an undecided dies and they are a different story. It is seldom, most people die having made their decision about God, but on this occasion, they died undecided. On these occasions both the angels and dark ones are dispatched while heaven makes a determination on the fate of the soul. Dark ones like to get there first, at least to detain the soul, even if ultimately, they have to relinquish it to God. In the case of Amy and Johnathan, the latter was true but with a small twist. An angel, their guardian angel, was already present and in possession of their souls...sort of. And he was 'sort of' their guardian angel...let's move on.

Amy was still whining as she came up the hill, unaware of the two figures gaining ground on her. Leahcim waved his arms and in a hushed voice said, "Stop! Don't move. Be quiet!"

She looked up and saw Johnathan and Leahcim waving and motioning for her to be quiet. Right then she felt them come upon her. A very dark presence enveloped her. Her heart began to race as she imagined a bear or a werewolf, that's the kind of mind she had. She froze, as she could feel their panting breath on either side of her.

Dark ones, or the gatherers, have a very poor sense of both hearing and sight, they do however have a very keen sense of smell.

The dark ones were standing beside her now, with their noses up and moving their heads from side to side sniffing the air for any scent of a human. Which is ironic in a sense, because the very smell of a human triggers a violent gag reflex in them and they nearly vomit at the smell. (And very often do.)

Amy closed her eyes, she could feel its hot breath on her cheek as it sniffed. With a huff and a loud grunt, they slowly moved away from her, sniffing the air as they went and disappeared into the fog. Leahcim and Johnathan ran down the hill to meet her.

"It's ok," Johnathan said as he reached her. "They're gone."

"What was that? And who is he?" She asked, voice trembling. Amy, seeing Leahcim said, "Who are you? Do you have a mirror? Somebody tell me what is going on!" They both were looking at Leahcim.

"We have to be quiet," he said, and began to explain. "They were dark ones."

"What are dark ones, and what do they want?" Johnathan asked.

"You." Leahcim answered. "They're here for you... well your souls anyway."

"Our souls!" Amy said, in a condescending tone. "How rude, we're not even dead yet!"

"You better tell her," Johnathan said.

"Tell me what?"

"Right." Leahcim said. "Well, here's the thing Amy. It appears that someone... made a mistake. Well... me, I made a terrible mistake, and you are in fact...," he swallowed hard, "dead."

"What?" Cried Amy. "I am not dead! I am way too rich, and way too popular to be dead. And besides, my father would never allow this!" She whined. "And I'm really pretty. And...," she began to weep, "Dead people aren't pretty. There are no pretty dead girls. Oh and my father is...," she began, but stopped. As she looked at Leahcim she saw a familiar face in him and his dirty clothes. All smelly and with that small leather pouch tied around his waist. Her memory flooded back to her. She was seven or eight years old, with her father guiding her by the hand, they were getting out of his car. The chauffer was holding the door for them, and they were walking to his office, the tallest building in the whole world. Her daddy's office was on the very top floor, she could see the whole world from up there. And she knew her daddy ran the whole thing, the world that is.

As they walked toward the door a beggar approached them and said, "God bless you, can you spare some change for coffee?" Her father had brushed him aside and looked down at her and said, "We don't give money away to anyone sweetheart. God's not going to bless us for helping someone who won't help themselves." That was the only time in her life she had ever heard her father mention God. As they approached the door, Amy looked back into his old eyes and he had smiled at her. She never saw that man again. On occasion over the years she would remember him and always wondered what he had kept in the small leather pouch.

Leahcim also remembering, saw what she had remembered, and said, "I've been assigned to the two of you for a long time, since your births really. My trainer and I have had many interactions with the two of you."

"Your trainer?" Johnathan said.

"Yes," Leahcim said, "I'm not officially your guardian yet, but I'm very close... at least, I was."

"Wait," Johnathan said, "So you're not even an angel yet!?"

"Well, I am an angel. I'm just not done with training yet. Today was my final exam, sort of."

"I think ya got an F, pal."

"And this whole thing is your fault?" Amy said.

Leahcim rushed to explain, in a condensed version, how it really wasn't his fault. And that it all came down to his robe getting caught in the escalator, but it would be all right. Everything would be all right, they just had to wait, and as soon as the trial was over heaven would reopen. And then they would ascend the escalator and figure this whole thing out. He hoped.

Johnathan sat down on a rock, elbows on his knees head in his hands. "You caught your robe in the escalator?"

"Yes," Leahcim said.

"If you're an angel, and those other things are demons, then where is God?"

"I'm not sure, I can't seem to reach him right now." Leahcim stated sadly.

"You can't reach God." Johnathan said incredulously.

"I think it's because He's in court today. The whole trial thing."

"Gods in court? Is he being sued?"

"Oh dear me, no! He's the judge. Lucifer has brought allegations against someone."

"Lucifer as in the devil?" He said, doubtfully.

"Yes, that's right."

Amy interrupted, "If I'm really dead, I think we need to take some time and mourn my loss. I mean the loss of me! And we should stand over my body and say nice things about me! This is a huge social tragedy, and no one will ever be the same."

"Shut up Amy! You're really dead! Live with it!" Johnathan shouted.

Amy said, "I don't believe either of you, this is not how rich people die."

"Oh really Amy?" Johnathan said. "How do rich people die?

"They die surrounded by all their stuff and butlers and staff and family members waiting for their inheritance." Amy said.

"What? Are you kidding?" Johnathan said, rolling his eyes. "All I know is I wouldn't be dead if I hadn't been driving you to the airport, so that you could go to your stupid class reunion! Which isn't even real, because you never even went to high school, your nanny went for you!"

"She only went on test days," Amy said.

"And besides who is ever going to use math, *ever* in their lives when you have a smart phone? Hello!"

"Oh and by the way Amy, I quit!" Johnathan said. "As of right now I no longer work for you, or your stupid father! And you can tell your father I'm glad I wrecked his car... the other one I mean. And I'm not going to pay for any of it, or this one either!"

Johnathan used to drive for Amy's father as his head chauffer. One morning on the way to his office, a taxi pulled in front of Johnathan and hit his brakes. Johnathan couldn't stop in time and slammed into the back of the taxi cab, causing Amy's father to spill a rather hot latte all over his five thousand-dollar Armani suit. Her father, as punishment, demoted Johnathan to the lowest, most feared and most loathed position he could think of, Amy's driver. Amy had had five other drivers over the past sixteen months, all of whom had disappeared. It was rumored among the other staff members that she had killed them all and buried them in the lake behind her father's house. None of which was true - the fact was, they all quit without notice, and just slipped into the night and were never seen or heard from again. Not surprising really. Amy had a very sharp tongue, and a mouth that could make a sailor run from the room in tears. In short, Amy was a mean, foul mouthed, rich kid who took great pleasure reminding the rest of the human race just how far down the food chain they really were.

The two of them went on and on...finally Leahcim shouted "Stop! We need to be quiet, the dark ones could be anywhere and if they find us, I don't know what will happen. We need to just sit down over there in the trees and wait."

"Can Johnathan at least go to the car and get all my suit cases?" Amy asked. "I can't take this smell anymore and I really need a mirror."

"Get your own suit cases," Johnathan quipped.

"No," Leahcim answered, "I think that smell is what saved you from those two dark ones. I don't think they could smell you because of the poop." He said. Amy sank against a tree.

"How long do you think it will be?" Johnathan asked.

"I'm not really sure," Leahcim answered. "This has never happened before... an angel getting stuck on earth that is."

"Well can't you teleport yourself back to heaven or something?"

"No," Leahcim said. "I've been trying while you two were fighting. I tried to think myself home, and nothing happened. In heaven, we can think of a place anywhere in heaven and we're there. To get to earth we use the escalator and when we reach the bottom you're just there were you need to be, instantly. This is different, I can't explain it."

"Don't they send you with a cell phone, or a mirror or something?" Amy said, snarkily.

"Stop with the mirror Amy!" Johnathan shouted.

"I meant to signal with ape!" She was lying, she really wanted a mirror.

Leahcim's face lit up. "The manual! We have a manual and the pouch of stones!" He took the pouch from his waistband and opened it. Amy sat up and looked on with excited eyes. He spilled the contents on the ground. There was a small book and five small stones, all of which were similar except one, it was red in color.

"That's it?" Amy said. "Your rock collection and a pamphlet? Ugh!" She sat back down with a thump.

Leahcim sat down and began to read. On the front of manual in large letters it said, WHAT TO DO IF... He thumbed through each page.

"Anything?" Johnathan asked.

"Not yet," Leahcim answered. "Wait! Here it is," he began to read out loud. "You've missed the third bell to return and now you are trapped on Earth." He looked up and smiled at them, and then continued. "You're in BIG trouble! Oh dear!" He took a deep breath and returned to reading. "There is only ONE way to return to heaven. You must get to the emergency porthole, located in the eye of the needle. Once there, cast the red stone into the eye of the needle, and the emergency porthole will open."

"Eye of the needle?" Johnathan said, "Where is that?"

"The eye of the needle," Leahcim said in a discouraged voice, "is in Jerusalem."

"Massachusetts?" Amy asked.

"Israel, you idiot! Not Salem!" Johnathan shot back, rolling his eyes. "High school reunion," he said, shaking his head. "What is the eye of the needle exactly?"

Leahcim explained that thousands of years ago, there was a great wall that surrounded the city of Jerusalem. There were large gates that people, horses and wagons, and camels would go through to trade their goods, or enter the city. At night the gates were closed, and a small gate on the side of the wall, was the only way to enter after dark. This door was only large enough for one man. "The Son described this gate as 'the eye of the needle', you know...," he looked at them expectantly. "A camel and the eye of the needle?" he said, waiting for it to register with them. "It's easier for a camel to go through the eye of a needle than it is for a rich man to enter heaven!?"

They both had blank expressions on their faces. "Never mind," he said. "The problem is," Leahcim continued, "is that part of the wall doesn't exist anymore. And I don't know how we can cast a stone through a gate that doesn't exist. Oh my," he said, "Oh my."

CHAPTER 2
Angels, Demons, And You

There are literally hundreds of thousands of angels. Some minister to God day and night, and many serve in the army of God. And others serve as guardian angels, sometimes as many as up to three for every person on Earth. There are ministering angels, and messenger angels. Gabriel, for example, delivered some of the most important messages in history.

In God's Army there are generals, lieutenants, captains, and so on. In the hierarchy of angels, Leahcim would rank as a guardian angel in training. The personalities of angels are much like that of humans, each one has their own little nuances and characteristics. Obviously, things that define them as individuals - some are very serious, others are funny. Some are very rigid and stick to the rules, and some a little bit aloof and like to bend the rules. Leahcim was different, he was a rather large angel, and somewhat clumsy, and (some would say) easily distracted by say, oh... a butterfly or a blue car. He wasn't slow or dim-witted, he was just, ...well, Leahcim. Always fascinated by God's creations, he'd sometimes spend hours studying the intricate design of a snowflake, or how a tiny seed can be turned into a plant and then grow into a piece of fruit. These things fascinated Leahcim. He always thought that, because of his rather large size, he would be a wonderful candidate for the army of the Lord. But then he really didn't like confrontation at all, and he was perfectly happy being a guardian angel in training. It was a very big responsibility after all. God himself assigns each angel to their task, and they do only what God gives them to do. Nothing more and nothing less. It is a very serious task and requires absolute concentration to even the smallest of details, as it is a very serious matter. Their job in a nutshell, is to bring glory to God. They are to watch after his children, to interfere when necessary and directed to do so. They will fudge, nudge or influence when they need to. After all these are God's children, and he wants them back, and will go to any lengths to achieve this. But NEVER, under any circumstances, are they to interfere with, or try to change free will.

Dark ones are just as diverse as angels, all are nasty, ill-tempered, angry drones subject to Lucifer's every whim. There are gatherers, such as those currently in pursuit of our three friends. There are armies of the dark, they fight angel's day and night. For example, a prayer is uttered by a believer on earth, God hears the prayer and dispatches an answer. The armies of the dark will wait for the angel and hold him up and delay the answer for as long as possible. The messenger angels will fight off these demons, and generally speaking will defeat them. On occasion an angel of the army of God has to come to the aid of the messenger angel to help. Michael for example, God's Archangel has had many battles with the dark ones.

Lucifer's goal in all this, is to keep as many humans as he can from ever believing in God. To steal as many souls as he can, before time runs out. Lucifer is not omnipresent as God is. He can't be everywhere like God can, which makes him and his demons opportunistic bottom feeding rats! They will whisper into the ears of believers and non-believers alike. In the ears of believers, they'll whisper things like, 'God doesn't really love you because you did that thing.', or 'Now you've done it, God's going to punish you for that one.' Or, 'Your wife will never know.'

If Lucifer can cause a believer to stumble and take the bait he's dangling in front of them, he can make them ineffective instruments to bring others to God. Although he can't change the fact that they are going to heaven.

One of his favorite targets are preachers, bring one of them down and countless others will doubt and never commit. Lucifer loves this.

When he can pit believers against non-believers, or believers against believers, or better yet... spread a false doctrine wrapped in a little truth, then that was just enough to keep them from ever knowing the truth.

Johnathan was the victim of one of these whispers, and he believed the lie he was told years ago. A whisperer had told him, after attending church one morning with his grandparents, that what the pastor had said about God wasn't true. That He was angry with sinners and He was sending them all to hell, for all sorts of reasons. That meant that he would never make God happy and that he would never qualify for heaven. He didn't understand what he had done to make God so mad at him, but he was certain God loved everyone except himself, Johnathan. So he spent all these years since his childhood avoiding God. After all, if God was mad at him and was going to send him to hell, then Johnathan wanted nothing to do with him.

In the ears of non-believers, it can be much more violent and well... evil. Things like "kill him," "pull the trigger" or "rob the bank, you'll never get caught". Picture in your mind a parking lot late at night, and a group of men in a circle. In the center of the circle an innocent man stands trembling, in front of him, a much larger man, holding a knife. The two are moving in a circular motion. Now, picture ten or twenty demons unseen by men, all circling them chanting "stab him, stab him, stab him". Just like rabid dogs in a frenzy, sometimes get so excited they break into violent fights among themselves, tearing at each other's flesh with their razor-sharp teeth. Well, finally the larger man lunges, and well...you get the picture.

I should also add that the dark ones are just as tenacious as those dogs, in their effort to prevent God's will from being achieved. They will cause doubt, or they'll lie, cheat, steal, or rob, murder, rape, or pillage. Or in some cases they will make themselves look like an angel of light, or even sound like the voice of God... whatever it takes to keep people from the truth. You see, Lucifer knows his time is about up, so he must steal as many souls as he can before the clock no longer ticks, and time's up.

Lucifer believes in himself, he believes he is god, and that he will overthrow God's kingdom. He thinks he will sit on God's throne, and everyone will worship him. So, it's a numbers game to him, the more souls he steals, the more worship he will receive. If you could only see what's beyond our vision all around us! The angels and demons are there constantly... and the battle that wages day and night between the two, would blow your mind. The literal millions of good and evil angels and demons, both carrying out their assignments by pitting themselves against each other in a fight for your very existence. I think you would scarcely be able to get out of bed from the fear of it all.

Amy was an easy subject for Lucifer. He really didn't have to spend a lot of time on her. She already believed that her biological father was god, after all, he provided everything she ever needed, her past, present and future was taken care of. People were mostly an inconvenient necessity to be used for what they could offer her in the moment... and then tossed aside and on to the next one. She was the perfect subject, never a threat to Lucifer. The chances of Amy ever causing anyone to believe in any god, other than hers, was virtually impossible. Still, there was this very small, very dim light, way down in the smallest corner of her soul. A light that if fed, had the possibility of growing into a raging flame. Lucifer was about the only one, besides God, who could even *see* this tiny little light, but it was enough to keep Lucifer on guard. It was really quite easy for him, to keep her distracted with new things, or things she didn't have, like a new car, a new vacation spot, or a new facebook post about those new things...simple enough.

A few words about subjects, there are really three kinds of subjects. Believers who are willing to listen, and actually eager to hear the voice. Non-believers, who refuse to listen, and just pass off any of those types of thoughts or voices as nonsensical or irrational thoughts. And then there are the undecided.

While most of them are willing to believe at some level, they have the hardest time getting past their own egotistical, self-centered and self-righteous personalities. The thought that the world does not revolve around them is just something that they cannot fathom. This could be and should be said about the human race in general.

Now, angels are involved in the lives of all of these, believers, non-believers and undecideds, as are the dark ones. Believers are a complicated lot, although they believe, they need a lot of interaction. It's easy for them to become distracted by their own thoughts and actions. They tend to interject their ideas, and try to make them God's ideas, and it can get just plain messy. Don't get me wrong, God gave humans a brain and a life. And he expects them to use them by pursuing their desires, wants, dreams, jobs, etc. The issues arise when seeking God's will for their lives, well they can get a little zealous. They over think everything, and Lucifer doesn't help with his whisperers running around planting all the doubt, confusion and nonsense that he can.

If they would just do what God told them "Be still and know that I am God" much of their problems and confusion would just evaporate like a cloud!

The angel's job is to watch over them, protect them, move them, inspire them, and reassure them.

Unbelievers are not as hard, they just need proof. Rock solid, unshakeable, scientific, undeniable proof. When it can't be proven by science or math, or the internet, then it must not be true. God interacts with these folks Himself. Drawing them in, proving Himself, slowly and methodically over time. He will move in and out of their lives, some notice and come to Him, some don't. Lucifer spends a lot of time on these people, if they don't believe, then they pose no threat. Just a subtle reminder every now and then about how ridiculous this theory of creation is, and that suffices for quite a while. And given enough time, he'll win.

Angels are mystified at the level of self-absorption these beings display and why God has such an obsession with them. They rarely even consider Him in their daily lives, and He is always the first one they blame and the last one they thank! And yet, He wants them, with Him forever...go figure.

And now that brings us back to the undecided, specifically Johnathan and Amy...these two were at best, difficult. Amy, a five foot eight-inch-tall, blond haired, blue-eyed beauty who was full of fire (and full of herself). And Johnathan, standing at five feet, eleven and a half inches tall (he describes himself as a solid six foot one) was timid for his size. He had dark hair and hazel eyes. A good looking young man, but not at all sure of himself. The next few weeks would change both of them forever.

CHAPTER 3
Make A Run for It

Back to Johnathan, still sitting with his head in his hands. And Amy still whining about her tragic and most untimely death. They both began to feel the weather change. A stiff wind had begun to blow, and the smell of rain was in the air. South Texas this time of year can go from sunshine, to rain, to an ice storm in a matter of minutes. A crack of lightning lit up the night sky, and then a down pour of rain came quickly after. The three ran for a small barn, a few hundred feet away.

Inside and soaking wet, and finally somewhat cleaned of the cow dung, they sat down on a pile of loosely strewn hay. It smelled of cow manure and mold. But, it was out of the rain, and for that they were thankful. Amy began to question Leahcim.

"What now?" she asked.

"I'm not sure," Leahcim responded.

"You said we had to go to Salem or something."

"Jerusalem, you idiot!" Johnathan shot back.

"Whatever. Do we fly there, or take a car or what?"

"Oh my g..." Johnathan started, shaking his head.

Leahcim, still not entirely sure what to do, said, "There are a lot of things we still don't know. Like, how dead are you? I mean are you *fully* dead, or are you just *kind* of dead? Or maybe you're not dead at all, and this was just part of my training, you know... like a test." With that he reached over and slapped Johnathan across the face.

"Ow!" Johnathan screamed, "why did you do that?!"

"See there," Leahcim said. "Now if you were alive, my hand should have gone through you, but it didn't. On the other hand, if you were dead ...you shouldn't have felt anything."

"What the hell does that tell us!" Johnathan quipped.

"Wait!" Amy said, "Angles fly everywhere right?" She paused for a split second, "You fly around at night giving little kids money for their teeth, so it's simple then. We just get on your back and you fly us to whatever that place is we're supposed to go."

"Oh, you're such an idiot, that's the tooth fairy you moron! He's not the tooth fairy!"

"The point is he can fly, Slumdog!"

"STOP," Leahcim shouted. "I can't fly. We move by thought, or by direction given from above. You're thinking of the Armies of the Lord, Archangels and Cherubim's and such, they're a different class of angel. I'm just an angel in training... I'm not fully empowered yet."

"We are so screwed," Johnathan said.

"The point is," Leahcim said, "I'm not sure exactly what your status is. The fact that dark ones have gotten wind of you means you're up for grabs. And if they get their hands on you, it could be... well, really, really bad. We have to avoid getting caught, so don't leave my side no matter what! Stay next to me. I can protect you as long as I can see you... I think."

Amy rolled her eyes.

"Dark ones," he continued, "these types are gatherers. They are sent out to gather lost or undecided souls. They can't see or hear very well but they can smell a human soul miles away. And they're nasty, mean little boogers. So stay right next to me."

"You keep saying undecided," Amy said. "Undecided about what?"

"Whether or not you believe."

"So, you mean... in God?"

"Yes."

"And if we do believe, what happens then?"

"Heaven," Leahcim said.

"And if we don't?" she asked.

"Then the dark ones take you," Leahcim answered.

"So, you're here to escort us to see God, and people in heaven? So they can decide where we go?"

"Yes...something like that. As I said, it doesn't usually happen this way."

"Then you need to send Johnathan to the car to get my bags, if I'm meeting people from heaven I need to change," Amy said haughtily.

"First of all," Johnathan said, "get your own bags! And second of all, you're not going to a talent show you brat! And third, *NO!*"

Amy turned to Leahcim and said, "Will you tell that trailer turd over there, that I'm not leaving this barn until I have clean clothes and fresh makeup? Once these people see me, they'll realize who I am, and what a major mistake has been made. Then I'll get my body back, you'll be demoted to elf or something, and he," motioning to Johnathan, "can go back to his trailer and continue doing whatever it is trailer turds do!" she yelled.

"Oh if we ever get back...," Johnathan started.

Leahcim cut him off, "Johnathan, will you please get her some clothes, so we can move on."

Johnathan shook his head and said angrily, "One bag, snot girl, you get one bag."

"Make sure it's the big one, and make sure it has everything I need. And be sure it's not covered in cow poop, and..."

Johnathan put his finger over his mouth and said, "Shut up, just shut up."

He opened the barn door and looked out, the rain had subsided to a light drizzle. He stepped out into the cow pasture. He was cursing Amy under his breath as he slipped and slid through the mud and cow pies, down towards the car. He could hardly see through the darkness and the drizzle, he squinted, and thought he could make out the vague outline of the car. As he got closer, he could see that the car had landed on its wheels, the trunk and doors were all open, and Amy's luggage was strewn all over. All of them were open, clothes, shoes, makeup were everywhere. Just then he tripped on something. He looked down - it was Amy's body!

"Eew! Gross!" he said. He stopped to look at her and bent down and turned her over. She looked kind of peaceful, her eyes were closed, and her face was covered in cow manure. He realized this was the first time he had ever seen her, when she wasn't screaming or whining...it made him a little sad.

Suddenly his thoughts were broken when he heard a rustling from the other side of the car.

A dark one appeared, then another, and another. Johnathan began to back up and tripped again over Amy's body. He fell backwards onto his butt, his heart was beating fast as he started to scramble back up the hill on his elbows. The dark ones where all over the car now, it looked like at least 20 of them. They were jumping and hitting it with their long arms, grunting and biting at each other. He could see more coming out of the forest, as he got to his hands and knees and scrambled up the hill to the barn. He hit the door hard and landed on his rear. It was locked. He began hitting it with his fist, Amy was on the other side.

"Do you have my bags?" she asked.

"Open the door, they're here," he said in a loud whisper. "The dark ones are coming!"

"Not until you say you have my bags, at least the big one with my makeup and mirror," she said.

"Amy," Johnathan said, his voice had a slight shaking in it. "If you don't open the door right now, I'm going to personally feed your tiny little pea brain to the dark ones! Now *open* the door!" She opened the door.

"Dark ones," Leahcim said. "How many?"

"I don't know, a dozen or so," he said shakily.

"We have to make a run for it, now while it's still raining," Leahcim said.

"Run where?"

"Anywhere...fast, away from here! They'll smell us out at any minute, we have to go."

The three left the barn quickly and headed out away from the car across the fields.

They walked for what seemed to be hours, and now the sun was starting to rise. They had walked over endless fields, crossing fences and ditches, and trudging through mud and stickers. Amy saw it first, the lights in the distance. She could make out a small town, and she could see some buildings.

"A town," she cried. "I hope they have a Nordstrom, or at least a Saks." She took off running. "Come on we're saved!"

Johnathan and Leahcim followed. As the three entered the small-town, Amy was still ahead of the other two. She spotted a church and yelled back at the others, "Hurry, a church, and there's people too. Maybe they can call God for us."

She bolted across the street, and before Leahcim could warn her, she was at the front door. Half way in, she turned to motion for them to hurry. Suddenly, she was ripped violently inside, and the door slammed shut behind her. The two of them ran across the street and burst into the front door. There, in the middle of the lobby, was Amy, two dark ones had her by either arm. Tears were running down her face and her eyes were closed. They forced her to her knees. She was shocked at how they felt kind of slimy and cold to the touch. She was terrified. When they saw Johnathan and Leahcim, the two dark ones looked at each other bewildered. One let go of Amy and stomped angrily across the lobby floor, the wood floor breaking under his feet with every step.

"Aaarrrrr," he growled as he reached Leahcim. "Why are you here White one! You're not supposed to be here today." His face was nose to nose with Leahcim. He huffed and sniffed at Leahcim's face, then he leaned over to Johnathan and sniffed him, and then he gagged violently.

"These are not yours, they belong to us," he growled. "You have no claim to these two. Today is ours, white ones are banned today."

Leahcim winced at the smell of the demon's breath. It smelled like a mix of rotten fish and vomit. These two demons were not gatherers, they were whisperers, assigned to this church. They would walk up and down every isle of the church, seeking out new or weak believers. Even seasoned believers were their targets. They would whisper in their ears as the pastor or priest was giving his sermon. "Don't believe him...," or "this is so stupid...," or "he's not talking about you, you'll never make the cut here," or "these people are not like you, you've done some really bad stuff He'll never forgive that." However, their weakness was during praise and worship, they would always make a point of leaving the church before praise started.

Singing to God in worship burned through them like a knife inside their head. Lucifer, before he was cast out of heaven, was the worship leader in heaven. All the worship would come from the angels in heaven and across Lucifer's desk, and he would pass the worship on to God. But that wasn't good enough for him, he had wanted all the worship for himself. So he planned a coup in heaven to take God off his throne, and steal all the worship for himself. He convinced a third of the other angels that they should join him and together they would rule heaven.

Well that didn't work out as planned, and he and the rest of the rocket scientists of heaven were cast down to earth forever - banned from returning and destined to eternity separated from the very God who created them. Therefore, worship being the very thing that got them cast down to earth, it was banned from Lucifer's realm. It also caused extreme pain in the ears of any who heard it.

Inside the sanctuary, in the very front row sat a very tiny black woman named Neli Grant, a ninety-seven-year-old sweetheart of a woman. Neli was at every church service, every Sunday, every week for the last seventy-seven years. She never missed a service, not once in seventy-seven years. She stood four feet, seven inches tall, and weighed all of 94 pounds. Today, she wore a blue dress, blue shoes, and a pearl neckless around her tiny neck. Her lipstick looked like she had put it on in the dark, and her blue eye shadow looked like it was put on by a professional painter.

As Neli was listening to the pastor speak, a strange urging took ahold of her, her spirit was becoming restless. She felt a terrible urgency to leave the sanctuary and go to the lobby, and she hadn't left during a sermon - ever! She made sure on Sunday mornings not to drink too much coffee. And she always used the lady's room before service so she wouldn't have to get up during service. But this was different, it was an urgent restlessness. She picked up her cane and began moving up the aisle toward the lobby, her cane made a clicking sound every time it would touch down on the floor. Click, step, click, step, up the aisle she went, click... click... click... click. She felt an overwhelming desire to sing. It kept building and building with every step she took, and she thought it would burst out of her. Click...click...click, as she kept walking she began to hum. Hmm hmm hmm hmm amazing grace was the tune coming out of her, click... click...click.

The demons were looking at Jonathan and Leahcim, their long ears began to twitch, just a little at first, click...click...click. Then they began to swat at their ears, like they were brushing away an annoying fly. Suddenly they all heard her coming, click click clicking and humming hmm hmm hmm hmm hmm hmm. It was getting louder and closer. Now the demons and our three friends were all looking toward the door to the sanctuary. Neli stopped at the door and looked up at the usher who opened the door for her, she smiled at him and began to hum again. There was a long silent pause when they saw the door to the sanctuary open, and then click, click, click and Neli

~ 37 ~

appeared. The demons drew their heads back at the sight of this little old lady. Neli made her way across the room to the center of the lobby, the only sound to be heard was the click, click, click of her cane on the hard wood floor. She stopped and turned, facing the five of them, she drew a long breath filling her lungs with as much air as they could possibly hold. And then, as loud as her little voice could, she began to sing. Her voice cracking and shaking with every word, way off key and way out of tune, she began, "*Amazing grace, how sweet the sound... that saved a wretch like meeeee... I once was lost, but now I'm found, was blind but now I seeeeee...*" At this, the demons began growling fiercely. They grabbed their ears and fell to the ground, clutching their ears and screaming. Rolling back and forth on the ground, the agonizing pain was unbearable!

Leahcim looking at this four-foot, seven-inch giant, he knew what this meant and smiled from ear to ear. "Let's go," he said. Johnathan grabbed Amy's hand and they ran towards the door. Amy looking back at the little woman dressed in blue, still singing as loud as she could. They flung open the door, half ran down the steps, and moved quickly down the sidewalk.

Neli kept singing even after she saw the doors to the church fly open and then slowly close. She heard the congregation begin to sing in the sanctuary, Amazing grace. Oh, she didn't want to miss this. She looked at the front door to the church, and said, "Ok then," and turned and walked back to the sanctuary. Click..., click..., click. The demons lay screaming on the ground, twitching and convulsing.

Chapter 4
Free Will

As the three of them walked quickly from the church, Leahcim still smiling, said "That was amazing!"

"What the hell just happened? Who was she?" Johnathan said.

"A believer," Leahcim answered. "A true believer."

"We were in a church, weren't they all believers?"

"Not necessarily," Leahcim answered. "Not all who claim to believe really do, or really are."

"How can you tell?" Johnathan asked. "I mean what makes her different?"

"This is so exciting," Leahcim began, "I thought I was all alone down here you know on my own, but then she showed up!"

"I still don't understand."

"She was obeying the Holy Spirit! She didn't just by chance show up and start singing. She was urged by the Spirit to do it, and she obeyed. And she probably didn't even know *why* she wanted to sing, but she did. It means we're not alone, it means the Holy Spirit is still here working, and there's hope and a plan."

"Ok," Johnathan said. Amy and Johnathan had that look on their face that says, 'we're listening but you're speaking Portuguese.'

"Look at the human race as a beautiful crystal vase," he started. "Sitting nicely on the shelf. Lucifer comes along and knocks the vase to the ground, shattering it into a thousand pieces. God comes with some glue and puts every piece back together perfectly. The Holy Spirit IS the glue. Without him holding it all together it would crumble again and fall apart. If he wasn't here, it would be total chaos, and we would be lost forever."

"Well, why don't you just talk to him, and tell him to take us back to heaven with him? And why doesn't he just talk to us, or you? Why send some wrinkly old lady who can't even sing?"

"He did talk to us," Leahcim said. "Through the old lady, He protected us."

"Let's find somewhere safe to hide for a while so I can read the handbook, maybe I missed something." They passed an abandoned building and ducked inside, it was old and smelled like dust and grease. They moved to some old mattresses spread out on the floor and sat down. Leahcim took out his manual and started reading.

Just then a young man slipped through the doorway, he was followed by a demon, and a whisperer. The three ran and hid behind a pile of shelving. The young man was talking to himself, "I don't want to do this anymore! I can't do this anymore! I'm so tired!"

The demon said, "You're so sick and this will make us feel so much better. One more time, it will be soo good, your gonna feel so much better. You'll just get sicker and sicker, you don't want to be so sick, just do it today and then we'll quit for good."

The young man looked up towards heaven and cried, "Help me!" He screamed and began to weep.

The whisperer said, "There's no one there to hear you. He doesn't care about you anyway. If He did, you wouldn't need this and besides this will be the last time. Tomorrow we'll get up and check into rehab, just this last time, one more hurrah. Your wife and kid will be so proud of you tomorrow, come on do it! You need this! You deserve this!"

With that the young man sat down on the dirty mattress and took the heroin from his pocket and began to prepare his needle. The demon began to laugh, "Haha yes! This is going to feel soooo good! You're going to love this!" The demon turned his head and vomited at the smell of the human. "Oh I hate you, you smell like God you weak little punk." He said under his breath, "*Do it!*"

The young man, with tears in his eyes wrapped a tourniquet around his arm, he put the needle up to the spoon and drew the liquid into the syringe. Then he stuck the needle into his arm, drawing the plunger back a little, his blood spilled into the syringe, and with a sigh he pushed the plunger into the syringe. He slumped back against the wall, the needle still hanging from his arm.

"Yes, yes, yes! You're such a fool!" The demon laughed and shouted, as he started dancing in circles skipping around the room. He looked at the young man and said, "Look at the bright side man, you can skip church this week!" He made his way out the door and disappeared down the street, still dancing until he disappeared from sight.

Leahcim came out from behind the shelves and walked over to the young man and sat down beside him. He put his arm around the young man and drew him towards himself. He began to stroke the hair above his forehead moving it out of the young man's eyes. Amy and Johnathan moved towards them.

"What's happening?" Amy asked.

"He's dying." Leahcim said without looking up.

Amy began to cry. "Do something!" She said.

"I can't," Leahcim said solemnly.

"Why not! You're an angel!"

"I'm not allowed to interfere."

"But, he's dying! You have to save him!"

"It's not allowed, Amy." His eyes filled with tears.

"WHY NOT?!" Amy demanded.

"Free will, Amy... Free will."

The young man breathed a heavy labored breath and slumped into Leahcim's arms. Amy began to sob. "What will happen to him?" Amy asked, "Will the dark ones get him?"

"Not this one," Leahcim said, still stroking the young man's hair. "He's a believer. He'll sleep until the angels come to gather him."

"So he'll get into heaven then? Even though he died this way?"

Leahcim finally looked up and with tears streaming down his cheeks said, "All of heaven will rejoice when he arrives, he will be welcomed and comforted."

Amy still sobbing, "Why didn't God save him, why did he just let him die? What kind of God let's someone die like that!?"

Leahcim answered "He did save him... a long time ago. We better move, that one will come back"

As Leahcim headed toward the door, Amy and Johnathan stood looking at the young man, the needle still in his arm. They both noticed the tattoo on the inside of his arm just below the needle, it was a circle of words that said FAITH=HOPE=FAITH=HOPE=. It hit the two of them hard, neither had ever witnessed a tragedy first hand like this. Johnathan shook his head and looked at the floor as he walked towards Leahcim. Amy had just experienced her first shot of

reality in many years... really in her whole life. This was something that moved her heart deeply, as she didn't think this sort of thing really happened. As she looked at the lifeless body of the young man, she wondered what his life was like before, before drugs? She thought about what the demon had said... 'your wife and kid will be so happy tomorrow'... her heart tore in two, she felt so hopeless and helpless. She had never had her heart broken before, she didn't like this. It made her feel real. She realized at that moment that she'd lived most of her life in a bubble, detached from the reality of life... from all of this.

"Amy, we have to go." Johnathan called for her from the doorway. The three left the building and stayed off the main street, moving down alley ways and side streets.

"I don't understand, "Johnathan began, "If that kid believed in God but did drugs, God still cared about him and will let him into heaven? I mean I thought you had to be perfect, I thought God only wants people who are squeaky clean and proper."

"If that were true heaven would be empty." Leahcim replied. He stopped and turned to the two of them and said, "All your acts of goodness and attempts at perfect behavior are like filthy rags, try as you might you can't earn your way into heaven. God wants you just as you are right now, broken. No matter how ugly and mean and vile you are, He loves you with all your faults... drug addictions, sex addictions, gambling, trust issues, love issues, pain, sorrow, fowl mouths, tattooed bodies. You are who He loves, the sick, the ones in *need* of a physician. It's when you come to Him that He begins to cleanse you and so tenderly love and change you, you can't, no matter how hard you try, clean yourself up completely. No one has ever come to their own salvation by their own hand."

They moved silently down the alley.

Finally, Johnathan asked, "Where to now?"

"Away from towns and people," Leahcim said.

"I'm really getting tired."

"You're tired?" Leahcim said.

"Yea I'm beat."

"That's great, the dead aren't usually tired." *More hope,* he thought. "Let's find somewhere to hide and you two can rest."

By now it was nearly dark, and Leahcim decided it would be safe to hide in the local thrift store. They would be closing soon and there wouldn't be any reason for the dark ones to come inside. They slipped in the front door as the last customer was leaving. The owner began shutting off the lights and gathered her items and she left for the night.

Amy hadn't said anything since the abandoned building. She went straight to the nearest couch, flopped down, and curled herself into a ball. She tucked a pillow under her head and was asleep in a matter of minutes. Johnathan found a blanket and covered her up.

Johnathan and Leahcim picked two recliners that faced the large window in the front of the store and sat down. Johnathan put his recliner back and kicked out his feet, and Leahcim did the same.

"I don't think I've ever been this tired." Johnathan said.

"You've never died before," Leahcim answered.

"No, I haven't."

"Except for that time when you stole your grandfathers boat, you came close that day."

"How do you know about that?"

"I was there."

"I almost drowned."

"I know."

When Johnathan was twelve, he spent the summer with his grandparents who had a home right on the beach in Corpus Christie, Texas. He and his grandfather used to go out onto the ocean and fish together every summer. Once, his grandparents left him home alone all day and Johnathan decided to take his grandfather's boat out by himself, something his grandfather had told him never to do. But, Johnathan was a stubborn twelve-year-old boy and he figured he could handle a short trip out and back before anyone knew.

He left the bay and made it out to the open water, then he decided he wanted to see how fast his grandfather's boat would really go. Grandad would never go full throttle, he would go just fast enough to keep the waves from coming over the bow. Johnathan pushed the throttle full forward until it couldn't go any further and zoom- the boat took off! Wow! The wind was in his hair and he was flying now! He sped around like a pro, as fast as the eighteen-foot outboard motor would go! He turned left, then right, then back straight, hitting waves head on full force! This was living! Then he turned the wheel hard to the right, just as a wave was swelling up. It caught the side of the boat and before Johnathan knew it, he was in the air, outside the boat flying through the air! Then splash, he hit the water hard. The shock of the chilly water and the trauma of being thrown overboard nearly stopped his young heart.

When he came up for air the boat was gone. It had straightened itself out and was speeding away full throttle, all Johnathan could see of it was the wake and the back of the boat disappearing into the distance. Johnathan began to tread water, turning in circles looking franticly for any sign of land, as the waves kept slapping him in the face. His heart was pounding out of control. First, he thought of his granddad, *what was he going to do?* Then his grandmother, *Oh no, they'll probably never let him come back to see them again, and granddad is going to be so mad...*Then back to reality, he was in real trouble with no life vest on, and miles from shore treading water. Reality set in quickly that he might die out here, and he began to panic. Instinctively he began to swim, as fast and as hard as he could.

Then he realized he didn't know which way to go? He stopped and turned and began swimming again in the other direction...face in the water, swimming, he began to cry. He stopped swimming and thought hard, he remembered that his grandad would tell stories of fisherman whose boat had capsized. How they would tread water for days before being rescued...he didn't think he could tread water that long. His heart sank at the thought of what he had done and how he ended up here. He wished so bad that he had just stayed home now. He floated and drifted for hours, he kept thinking a boat would come along or the coastguard would find him. He wondered if his grandparents where home yet, and if they had called a rescue team? Maybe they were already looking for him, maybe any minute he would be found.

He began to pray, "God if you're up there...please help me, please... I'll never do this again.
If you'll just send someone to save me, I'll be good for the rest of my life... I won't cheat on any more math tests or steal any more candy from Mr. Clark's store...I'll be really good!"

He thought about God, and how he had heard from that preacher once that all bad people go to hell. And that God only liked good people, and if you weren't like the other people in his church you would make God mad, and he would never let you into heaven. This didn't help much, because now he felt hopeless. He drifted some more. Johnathan began to get tired and his legs

were cramping. He started to panic again, he could barely tread water anymore and he began to sink. He made himself paddle harder, but his legs wouldn't work...he was drowning!

Suddenly the ocean started to bubble all around him, the water was churning and bubbling and rolling. It got louder and louder and more violent, as a huge black mass began to emerge from the ocean floor from underneath the water. It came up and up, getting larger and larger... a giant black metal monster was emerging from the water, and it pushed Johnathan aside as it rose. Then Johnathan saw on the side of the beast in white letters with an American flag, SS-13 STINGRAY. It was a submarine!

Suddenly sirens began to wail, and men were coming out of the top! He was saved! He couldn't believe it, *a real live submarine!* He began to scream and wave his arms frantically. He couldn't see that Leahcim was standing next to the Captain on the bridge of the great beast, smiling.

"I told the Captain to check his periscope that morning."

"You where there? You sent the ship?"

"I've been with you for a long, long time, Johnathan."

"God heard your prayer, not me. I was just doing what He told me to do."

"That was cool though, I mean, a SUBMARINE!! You know my grandfather wasn't even mad?"

"I know, and neither was God," Leahcim smiled. "You should sleep, I'll read and see if I missed anything." Leahcim took out his manual and began reading. As Johnathan made himself comfortable, smiling to himself, he pictured Leahcim on that ship...and God.

Chapter 5
Lucifer's Camp

Lucifer was sitting in a dimly lit makeshift office, in the back of a Walmart, in Cut Off, Louisiana. He liked setting up in department stores this time of year because black Friday was coming, and he wanted to be as close to the action as he could. Not to mention it was now his best time of year, it beat out Halloween by a long shot.

Smoking a large cigar, feet on his desk, he leaned back and grinned, "Oh the holidays," he said. He was a handsome fellow, kind of tall, blond hair and blue eyes. Nicely dressed, not at all what one might expect from the descriptions in the fairy tales about him. He really was a handsome devil. He liked the descriptions and pictures of himself that people had made of him, tall, dark hair, goatee and horns. He especially loved the red cape, tail and hooved feet. And the pitch fork was cool! No, if you saw a red caped, hooved foot, horned head, pitch fork carrying guy coming at you you'd run! He felt that a softer more traditional look would not trigger such a violent response. After all, deception was the name of this game.

He was contemplating how to get the church to endorse black Friday when one of his captains barged in.

"There's a white one here today!"

"What are you talking about?"

"A white one was seen with the two undecideds you sent us for. He has them with him in a church in Tekus."

Demons aren't much on conversation ever since the fall, they would much rather grunt, or growl their way to a point. Lucifer made this Captain nervous, so he tended to mix up his words when speaking with Lucifer.

"TEXAS you moron!"

"Yea that place, anyway a couple of whisperers saw him."

"They're wrong. No white ones today. I would know if there was a white one here, go away."

"They said the Holly Sprit was there too," he said cautiously.

"HOLY SPIRIT...SPIRIT! Not SPRIT! And he's always here, if he wasn't here my existence would be all gremlins and goblins all day having fun," he mumbled.

"Ok, yea him too I guess. But get this, instead of taking them and going back, they *ran* out the door and got away."

Lucifer started, "If there was a white one here and he's running on the ground...actually running...with two undecideds...," Lucifer paused in mid-sentence.

"Yes, boss?"

"... That would mean...," another long pause, "...he can't........," an even longer pause, as he could barely grasp the thought, ".......get back?" He looked at his Captain. "Why else would he be running?" He pondered and then said under his breath, "No, the idiots made a mistake. It must have been a third undecided... somebody messed up the file. But just in case... take a few guys and head to TEKUS and find these three. And by the way, what the hell is taking so long on this one? They should have been here yesterday, now go!"

The demon left, and Lucifer shook his head "Tekus... 'Holly Sprit'...I'm telling you! Every one of those guys hit their heads when we landed!"

Lucifer sat back down and began plotting again. As he plotted, his body began to change from the well-dressed handsome fellow into something else. The blond hair faded away, the blue eyes turned to coal black disks, and his body kind of just faded into a black mist that hovered around his chair, swaying with the slightest breeze. His real presence would freeze a preacher in his tracks, and send a nonbeliever running for a cross. He was pure, dark evil. He was the master of deception and the father of all lies...and he was good at it.

His weakness, that in the fall, he lost his ability to be everywhere. Angels and God can be anywhere and everywhere all at the same time in God's omnipresence. But Lucifer was confined to whatever he could focus on in any given moment. His other weakness is that although he can, and very often does, have the appearance of an angel of light, he can't sustain the illusion for very long. He likes to try to look and act like God in his efforts to deceive, but maintaining this illusion is not possible. So, he's forced to bounce back and forth from one task to the other. He spends a lot of time going back and forth from earth and heaven bringing accusations against God's people. He's always accusing them, he brings up every detail of their failures and puts them in front of God. On some occasions these end in trial, hence his demons have to do a lot of his work for him, while he is forced to focus on whatever manipulative deception is at hand at that moment. 'He roams the earth like a lion looking for whoever he can to devour', was a completely accurate description of him.

One of the tools in Lucifer's possession, that can only be used by a certain class of demons, is that they can throw themselves into the body of a non-believer. They use non-believers because there is no light in them. Lucifer being darkness, and God being light, the two can't occupy the same space. If there is light there can't be dark and if there is dark there can't be light, they are mutually exclusive.

These happenings are rare but can be very useful to Lucifer. To possess a human brings a lot of attention to the fact that Lucifer exists, and if Lucifer exits then God must too. So, they don't use this tactic unless they absolutely must. On occasion an overzealous demon will use a human to terrify someone. But all of his tactics are for one purpose and one purpose only... to keep you from believing in God.

He has practiced the art of deception for over 4 thousand years and has become the expert in it. Causing doubt and looking like God is a true art form. Building new religions, witchcraft, and cults with *just enough* truth in them to appear God like, *and* as harmless as possible, while plausible enough to believe in them, now that's art! All the while, distracting them from the truth long enough to let time expire on them. Yes, he has mastered his craft!

The Captain gathered 6 demons from the ranks and headed out for Texas.

Demons, like angels are a diverse group, some tall and skinny, some short and chubby, some just short with distinct personalities. Most are ill tempered, angry, and violent by nature, or due to their circumstances – being thrown out of heaven and all. They are loyal to Lucifer's cause, whether because they still believe that they will, at some point, rule heaven... or simply out of fear of Lucifer and reprisal from him, who knows. They go about their business with eager and resolute determination.

In a group, demons are particularly evil. They seem to work each other into an uncontrollable frenzy, which almost always ends up in them fighting each other. They relish destruction, feed off of fear, laugh at terror, and gain so much pleasure from the most gruesome acts of cruelty that man can subject his fellow humans to. Where Lucifer is exact in his planning and execution of a plan, these are a little more fly by the seat of their pants types. Intelligence isn't a qualifier in this group. Most don't like to speak, and contemplation of any situation or problem is usually forgone with just a good slap to the back of the head, from the one standing next to them.

Flight is not used, as their wings were singed off as they were cast to earth, and most of them just have nubs as the remainder of their wings. Most were deformed by fire, the feathers are gone but they still have dripping sores of pus, as they continue to rot away. Their arms grew longer, as did their legs. Their features are as different as they are, most are only similar in that they all turned a greyish white. This happened when they lost their life blood, which turned into a kind of greenish brown slime that runs through their veins and makes them cold to the touch.

Many suffered disfiguring injuries during the fall, and subsequent slam into the earth. They have broken legs and arms that never heal, twisted heads from broken necks, and ruptured spines that left many of them crawling on their stomachs. (They kind of just slither about dragging themselves with their arms.) None have any hair, their cheek bones protrude, and their teeth are green and rotting, and they all drool uncontrollably.

Their eyes are just grey, covered with a slime that causes them to water continually. Their hearing is terrible due to the same slime that drips from their eyes. The only sharp sense they have is that of smell, similar to that of a dog, they constantly sniff the air picking up clues and direction. When one of them picks up a scent it will scream in a hair-raising pitch which brings everyone running. Oh, and it's best to stay down wind of demons. On the ground, their long arms and legs propel them at amazingly fast speeds, running on all fours they can cover a lot of ground quickly. Out running one of these in a foot chase is all but impossible.

Their mode of transportation is whatever is at hand. They can just jump onto a train, car or boat, hang onto the tail of an airplane or ride on the wing. They are able to think their way into a space or place, just not with great accuracy. For instance, if they think *great wall of china* the odds are they'll crash land in the yellow sea, or if they're really lucky, slam face first into the side of the great wall. Unlike Lucifer, who has great control in his thought movement with pin point accuracy.

The six demons, with their Captain leading them, were moving fast, running with noses in the air, they should reach Texas by morning.

CHAPTER 6
These Are Not from God

It was 8 a.m. when Amy woke up. She had not moved all night, her sleep had been sound and deep. She had dreamt of heaven and clouds and being very peaceful but could not recall any of the details of her dreams at all. She slowly rose to her feet and stretched her back. As she looked around and realized her nightmare continued, she muttered, "Ugh, they haven't fixed this yet! What's taking them so long?" She looked over at Johnathan, still asleep in the recliner, and she walked by and purposely kicked the chair as she passed. Johnathan jumped and let out a little scream.

"Good morning. Planning on killing anyone today?" Amy said.

"What time is it?"

"I have no idea."

"Where's Leahcim?"

"Probably found something shiny in the back," she answered.

"That's not nice."

Just then Leahcim appeared carrying a pot of coffee and two cups. "I found some coffee in the back, and I thought you might like some." He smiled.

"Shouldn't we get out of here? She's probably opening soon." Johnathan said.

"No," answered Leahcim, "there's a sign in the window that says Closed Monday For Funeral. How did you sleep?" He asked the two of them.

"Weird dreams," Amy answered.

"Is there a bathroom back there?" She motioned to the back of the store.

"Yes just past the office." Amy headed in that direction.

"Did you sleep?" Johnathan asked.

"No, I don't need sleep."

"Ever?" Johnathan asked.

"We relax, rest would be a more accurate description, about every seven days."

Just then an ear-piercing scream came from the back room. The two bolted towards the sound, the bathroom door was closed, and Amy was locked inside, screaming.

"Amy open the door!" Johnathan yelled.

Amy threw open the door, "This!" she said grabbing her hair, "and this...," pointing at her face "is ALL YOUR FAULT!!!"

"What? You look fine."

"Fine...he said I look fine. I look like road kill, oh god I am road kill!" She began to cry.

"Look, there's clothes and makeup and stuff out here," Johnathan said nervously.

"Don't look at me," she said, covering her face. "Turn around! Don't look!" She pushed her way past the two very nervous men.

"Where are you going?"

"To dumpster dive in this...this...whatever this place is!"

This place was actually a very large thrift shop, in the center of town, with aisles and aisles of donated clothing, furniture, and housewares. Just the sort of place Amy and her friends would sneer at, and would never be caught dead in.

Amy angrily began looking at all the women's clothes. She was using two fingers to move from item to item, "Never!".... next item, "Never, never." next item... "Not in this lifetime!" this went on and on.

Johnathan and Leahcim moved to the center of the store and stood behind the counter, elbows on the glass top, head in hands, and watched. Leahcim heard it first, a rustling in the front of the store, near the door. Then Johnathan heard it, a kind of slapping sound, like someone slapping a piece of meat. Then a growl. They looked down the aisle and saw a dark one approaching, nose in the air sniffing. It's bare feet slapping the tile floor as it moved slowly up the aisle, stopping and sniffing. Then another one appeared, and then two more. They could see more a few aisles away.

Johnathan slipped around the counter, and on his hands and knees moved as fast as he could towards Amy. Reaching her, she looked down at him and said "Pig!"

"Get down!" He whispered, "Dark ones," he pointed at the door. She ducked down beside him. "Follow me," he said quietly. The two made their way back to the counter and slid in behind Leahcim.

"What do we do?" Johnathan asked.

"Be still don't talk."

Leahcim reached up to the counter and pulled a bottle of women's perfume off the display, and started dowsing Johnathan, and then he turned to spray Amy. She shook her head violently and whispered, "No!"

"Yes!" Leahcim said.

"No, never!"

"You must!"

Meanwhile, the dark ones were searching the store, two of them in the clothing department. One began putting on a women's coat and hat, and then looked at the other and started sashaying about said "Oooh look at me, I'm Amy, I'm soo rich and pretty!"

The other one grabbed a men's jacket and doing the same said, "I'm Johnathan, I'm stupid and I scream like a girl."

Just then one of the dark ones screamed from the center of the store. The rest jumped over racks of clothes, and tore through housewares and over furniture, moving quickly towards the scream. They had discovered Amy!

Amy and Johnathan were standing huddled together with Leahcim in front of them, blocking the Dark ones. They were surrounded on all sides of the counter. The Captain growled at Leahcim, drooling uncontrollably, vomiting at the very smell of Amy.

"You're not supposed to be here, White one. Lucifer will take this to God and accuse you, you'll be tried for this! These are his," he said, pointing to Johnathan and Amy.

Leahcim glanced at the two demons still dressed up and said, "I'm not here, we're not here. In fact, you have the wrong ones." Reaching into his leather pouch, he clasped one of the stones and cupped it in his hand next to him. He opened his hand slightly...

A spirit of confusion engulfed the demons. Leahcim pointed toward the two demons in clothes and shouted, "There they are! GRAB THEM!"

The two dressed demons began to growl and shake their heads in protest. The other demons pounced on them and wrestled them to the ground. They gagged them, tied their hands and stood them up. The Captain approached the one dressed as Amy, and as he stroked 'her' cheek said, "You're a pretty one, Lucifer will love you!"

With that, the demons turned and left the store, dragging the two captives behind them.

Johnathan stood with his mouth open, wide eyed and said, "What the hell?"

Leahcim dropped the stone to the ground and turned to Amy, "You must do as I say Amy, or they will catch us."

"Avon." Amy said. "Over my dead body!"

"Exactly," Leahcim said. "We have to leave, now! That will last until they get back to Lucifer, but it won't work on him, he's going to see right through it."

They ran toward the door, Amy grabbing a sweater off one of the racks as they ran by.

Back on the street they moved quickly, Amy pulled the red and green sweater over her head and said, "Eew so gross! This has to be hell."

The three made their way to the end of town. Amy, sort of stomping her feet said, "Can we just stop and talk somewhere? I don't get any of this. I mean, if I'm dead, why am I so hungry?" She whined, "And cold! And why is my hair so messy, and why would I care if I were really dead?"

Leahcim stopped. "I've told you I don't understand this either. You shouldn't be hungry, or ugly or tired."

"Nobody said ugly, I didn't say ugly, that's a little strong."

"We'll have to steal some food for the two of you."

"Can we do that?" Johnathan asked.

"Sure, why not?"

"Well, what if we get caught, or someone sees us?"

"You can't be seen or heard," Leahcim replied.

"But we can eat???"

"Apparently, if you're hungry, I imagine you'll be able to eat."

"So... what? We just walk into a restaurant, and start grabbing and eating stuff?" Johnathan asked.

"No, I would recommend a grocery store and a package of Twinkies. Or some muffins, maybe some lunch meat. And you'll have to eat it there, it wouldn't be good if people saw a package of lunch meat walking out the door on its own. Just eat as you move down the aisle ok?" Leahcim sighed, "And pay attention to people around you. They can see what you're touching or moving, they just can't see you. We don't want to cause a haunting, we just want a snack."

"There's a truck stop," Johnathan said, pointing down to the end of town.

"Oh even better!" Leahcim said. "We'll get a table in the back, and I'll manifest myself to the waitress, and you two can eat all you want. Just be careful, and sit close to me, when we're done I'll tell her the bill has been paid, and Boom, Bob's your uncle, and everybody's happy!"

"They can see you if you want them to?" Amy asked.

"Oh sure, people entertain angels all the time, they just don't know it."

"Have I?"

"You've seen me many times. And so have you." He said looking at Johnathan.

"When?" Johnathan asked.

"Do you remember that time when you were about 10 years old, and you lost all the money you had collected on your paper route? You dropped the bag you had the money in."

"Yes," Johnathan said solemnly.

"And that nice young woman found you sitting on the sidewalk, crying? She handed you the bag, remember?"

"That was you?"

"Yep, me." Leahcim smiled.

Amy asked, "What about me?"

"Well, I was the beggar outside your father's office that day... and let's see...so many times...Oh! Do you remember the maid you fired?"

"Which one?" She said, holding her hands out and rolling her eyes.

"You accused her of stealing your bottle of Chanel," Leahcim reminded her.

"Yes! That wicked troll said she didn't do it, and she reeked of it! I knew she couldn't afford Chanel, so she *obviously* stole it. She deserved to be fired! Wait, that was you?"

"No. But do you remember her son, the little boy who brought you some perfume later that day?"

"Yes."

"And he told you she hadn't stolen it, but she had broken the bottle. And she was afraid to tell you, and she just needed her job back. And you felt that little twinge in your heart, and you gave her her job back?"

"Yes, I remember."

"I was the little boy."

"So, you lied!" She said angrily.

"What?...No...You're missing the point." Leahcim said.

"Well what is the point? I got used by a five-year-old with a bottle of cheap drug store perfume, while I lost a $500 bottle of Chanel!"

"Your heart Amy, is the point, you know... that small black mass in the center of your chest?" Johnathan quipped.

"You're fired!" Amy shot back.

Johnathan pointed his finger at her and said, "Look you vixen..."

"Stop!" Leahcim shouted, "Let's just eat." He was shaking his head.

Outside the restaurant, Leahcim took the two to the side of the building and said, "I have to change, close your eyes." Johnathan closed his eyes. Amy rolled hers, and folding her arms finally closed her eyes. Leahcim grinned to himself as he manifested into a chubby little priest.

He said, "Ok, you can look now." Johnathan and Amy opened their eyes, "Well, what do you think?" he asked.

"You look like Friar Tuck," Johnathan said.

"I think you look like one of those fat penguins," Amy said.

"I'm a priest."

"Why so fat?" Amy said.

"You're hungry right? Who's going to deny a fat Priest?"

The three went inside and sat down at a table in the far corner of the café. The three of them squeezed into one side of the booth, one on either side of Leahcim. The waitress approached,
"Hello Father."

"Good morning my dear."

"Are you here for the funeral today?"

"No, just passing through."

"Oh, well maybe you should stay and help," she pointed out the window.

Leahcim turned and looked out the window. There were a large number of people gathering on the street with signs, a church group from another state. They were here to protest the funeral of the soldier who was being buried. Their signs were vulgar and mean, accusing the soldier of sinning against God. They said, God hated war and that all soldiers were sinners, with signs that said things like 'Your son is going to Hell,' and 'God hates murderers,' and 'Your son is a baby killer.'

The waitress looked at them and said, "I don't understand that kind of hate... I mean really...in God's name?"

"These are not from God," Leahcim said.

"Amen to that," she said. "What can I get you to eat, Father?"

Leahcim ordered enough food to feed half the town. The waitress smiled and said, "It'll be just a few minutes, Father." As they waited, Johnathan, Amy and Leahcim watched the growing group of protesters.

"Is that what God thinks?" Johnathan asked.

"No! Not even close!" Leahcim answered. "That Pastor lost sight of the truth a long time ago," he began. "Lucifer told him he was righteous in his beliefs and the Pastor believed the lie. So he stole God's righteousness, and put it on himself." Leahcim continued, "You see, man has no righteousness of his own. Not a single man, or women, in history has had a single ounce of righteousness that they could claim as their own. Only God has that claim. When you believe, you have His righteousness, not yours. The problem comes when some men and women try to put on God's righteousness and call it their own. Then throw in a little pride and swollen ego...and then there you go," pointing at the demonstrators. No, this is not from God, this is of their own egos.

"Why aren't there any dark ones with them?" Amy asked.

"Well, if you were a non-believer, and you saw these people representing God, would you want anything to do with a God like that?"

"No!"

"Lucifer," Johnathan said.

"The father of lies," Leahcim answered.

"There is one in the group that still knows the truth." Leahcim said, "And soon she will cause this flock to scatter."

"Why doesn't God stop them?" Amy asked.

"God's truth, no matter how turned around or twisted it may get, will always come back to the truth. This pastor, and all teachers of the truth are held to a stricter judgment. He will have to answer for this in the end. God is a just God above all else. As far as God's judgement on this soldier they're burying today, God himself said, "There is no greater love than that a man lay down his life for another.""

CHAPTER 7
Whistle While He Works

The three sat and talked for over two hours, watching the protesters, and formulating their plan to reach Jerusalem.

"We have to stay away from public places as much as possible." Leahcim said

"We can't swim to Jerusalem," Johnathan replied.

"No, but we can jump in cars and trains and make our way to New York, and then catch a boat and then more trains and cars."

"Why not just get on a plane? Or are you afraid of flying?" Amy asked.

"Airports will be full of demons, and imagine being caught on a plane, fighting a dark one at fifty thousand feet!"

"I think a train to New York is the best bet." Leahcim said.

"Well, let's find the train station and get a schedule." Johnathan said.

The three left the café and headed for the train station. As they walked, Leahcim began to give them some instructions about what to do when they saw dark ones, and how to fight them off.

"If they ever get ahold of you, just kick, punch, scream whatever you have to do to get away."

"You can punch a demon?" Johnathan asked.

"Sure, it's like hitting a cold piece of meat, but they feel it."

"Do they bleed?"

"Yah, a kind of green chunky slime and it stinks," Leahcim answered.

"Gross." Amy said.

They reached the station and found the schedule. There was a train coming through in an hour, and they would have to switch trains in New Orleans later that night. They sat outside on the other side of the tracks and waited. When the train finally arrived, Leahcim went on board and checked for dark ones, then returned and said, "Ok, there's four or five dark ones in the dining car at the bar, but I found an empty sleeping cabin toward the back of the train."

They made their way to the sleeping cabin and sat down. It was about a twelve-hour train ride from Texas to New Orleans. And now it was getting late again, and they were getting tired. They sat and watched out the window of their cabin as the train left the station.

Amy looked at Leahcim and asked, "So what's this God fellow like, is he nice?"

"Oh he's wonderful!" Leahcim replied.

"I thought he was mad at everyone." Johnathan said.

"No Johnathan, he's not mad at anyone. Lucifer started that lie." Leahcim sighed.

"He was mad once. Well not mad really, more frustrated than anything, I think." Leahcim tried to explain, "That was the day He, the Son, and the Holy Spirit, along with a few of the other angels, Gabriel and Michael, locked themselves in the throne room for almost a half a day. Which in the time span of earth, was about four hundred years," Leahcim continued. "He didn't speak to anyone on earth for four hundred years. No prophets were sent, no angles were sent... nothing! We all watched that day, a lot of things started happening. I think God just got fed up with all of you and decided it was time to send the Son."

"What happened?" Amy asked.

"Well, a lot of things went on that day. Heaven became a very busy place. We all knew of the events of the day, I mean we knew it was coming... we just didn't know it would be that day! And I don't think any of us were prepared for how emotional and powerful it was going to be." Leahcim paused. "Gabriel was busy delivering messages, the Holy Spirit was moving, and the Son departed..." Leahcim paused for a moment, his face became...sad. "And then something very strange happened," he continued.

"What, what happened?" Amy asked.

"Well after everyone had left, the throne room was closed, and we were all standing outside listening...waiting...all of heaven was silent. Not a sound throughout all of heaven...God was inside, alone for just a moment. And then we heard weeping from inside the throne room. I thought my heart would tear completely apart when I heard my Father weep...," a long pause, Leahcim with tears running down his cheeks, continued. "That was the saddest day of my existence and the happiest I've ever been all at the same time."

"Why?" Amy asked, "Why was God crying?" Amy asked with tears in her eyes.

"For his Son...for you..."

"Why, why would he cry for me?" Amy asked still crying.

"At the thought of losing you, you are always on his mind Amy... every day. He is always thinking of you."

"He had to turn away from His only son, only for a moment... and He placed all of the horror of mankind that had ever been done, past, present and future, onto him. All the ugliest things that man can do against man, and more importantly against God. Murder, rape, envy, strife, greed, lies, drugs, every horrible thing *ever* done, and placed it ALL on the shoulders of His son. And then He had to turn his back as all of that was nailed to the cross. All, so He could have you."

Leahcim went on, "We don't understand this, angels that is. We can't get our heads around this fascination He has with you. This obsession, that he would go as far as he did, to be with you." Leahcim looked confused.

"Anyway, it was just a few moments later and the doors to the throne room flew open. God stepped outside, and He spread His arms wide, looked up and drew a huge breath of air and said, "Thank me, it's finally over!" It was as if He had been a prisoner that was finally set free.

He turned to the Seraphim and told them to never close those doors again! And then the new covenant was in place, the old one was gone. Now everyone could come to the throne of God directly, no more goat blood, ox blood, no more sacrifices were needed, the veil was gone!"

"What do you mean?" Johnathan asked.

"The old covenant was very tedious and ritualistic. Goat blood, ram's blood, the blood of a bull, so much blood. It required daily sacrifices to provide forgiveness. The new covenant required only *one* sacrifice, and that was made by His Son. The old covenant was written on stone, but the new covenant would be written on your heart and requires nothing more than faith in the Son."

"Anyway," Leahcim continued, "God's attitude was different. I mean, he started whistling all the time, everywhere he went, no matter what he was doing he was always whistling. As soon as the Son returned, they started building the mansion. And there was God, swinging a hammer or sawing lumber and whistling the whole time!"

"God was working?" Johnathan asked.

"Oh yes, He's always working! He's a wonderful builder, I suppose that's where his Son gets it."

"Does he ever laugh? I mean does he have a sense of humor, is he funny?" Johnathan asked.

"He seems to enjoy it when someone gets bonked in the head unexpectedly or when they run into a closed glass door. When we all come together to give our reports, God watches the events of the day with us, and he loves it when someone runs headfirst into a pole or gets hit in the head with a bucket of fish chum. Not when they're hurt, but the silly ones that just shock them." Leahcim chuckled. "Consequently, angels do a lot of that, when you see someone get smacked in the head, or run into a closed door, it was most likely the doings of an angel."

Leahcim continued, "I've seen God laugh so hard he cried! You haven't heard a more joy filled robust sound than when the creator of all the universe laughs!! All of heaven stops what they're doing and just listens. And when he really gets going, and stomps his feet, all of heaven shakes. It's common knowledge that you don't start a game of chess, or jingo, during review time, He'll ruin your game if He gets going!" Leahcim was grinning from ear to ear.

"What's heaven like?" Johnathan asked.

"It's hard to describe with the limited words you have here. It's like here only in high def. When you see your shadow on the ground, you can tell it's you, but with no definition. Or the shadow of a tree without definition, earth is a type and a shadow of heaven, but really no words can describe the wonders of it. It's just not something I can put into words." Leahcim thought for a moment. "It is like the most beautiful spot on earth - times *TEN THOUSAND*. And nothing but joy there, no tears, no sorrow, no pain, no sickness. No evil of *any* kind, no Facebook, no twitter, no email.... Oh! And the stars! The moons, and the planets - the endless galaxy full of planets with stars and moons are just a playground reserved for later when everyone is home." His smile was huge now. "And the things He has created for later...." We angels don't even know the full scope of it all."

"Wait," Amy said, "No Facebook? How will people know I'm there? Or how will we know what someone else is wearing that day? Or who they're dating, or how much money they have?"

Johnathan reached over and grabbed Leahcim by the arm and said, "God has a plan, right? You said there is no evil in heaven, right?"

"You mean Lucifer?"

"No, her! He'll stop her right? Gag her or tie her up, or send her to another planet by herself, right?! I won't have to be with her right!? No-one should have to be with her! Leahcim..." Johnathan pleaded, "she's evil! I'm telling you God must have made a mistake!"

Amy folded her arms and huffed and stuck out her tongue at Johnathan.

"I'm going to go find you some food, don't leave the cabin," Leahcim said, "Ok? Promise you'll stay in here?"

"Yea, ok." Johnathan replied.

"Amy?" Leahcim looked at her.

"What?"

"You'll stay put?"

"Yes, I'll stay. You might wanna get some pudding for him though, because I doubt he'll have any teeth when you get back!" She shouted.

"You two need to try a little harder to get along. We have a long and hard journey ahead."

Leahcim then slipped down the corridor of the train toward the dining car. As he was walking, he saw a porter pushing a food cart from the kitchen, he was delivering a tray to another cabin.

The porter stopped and knocked on a door. "Just leave it outside please," came the answer from inside the cabin. The porter sat the tray down and left. Leahcim waited for the porter to be far enough away, and then picked up the tray and ran. As he entered the next car it was empty, with the exception of a single woman seated near the exit. He spotted a dark one standing behind her, leaning over the seat and whispering into the women's ear. He could hear the demon saying "They don't care, no-one cares. You would be so much happier if you were dead. All this pain would end... just do it!" The women was crying, tears streaming down her face. She looked out the window and thought *I have nothing left to live for. He's gone, I'm all alone!*

The demon started in again, "That's right, nothing at all to live for! And you could be with him again." She got up and moved toward the door of the train and walked out onto the platform. "Just jump," the demon said, "DO IT! JUMP!"

The women moved closer to the edge "Do it! Do it now! JUMP!"

Leahcim put the tray on the seat and moved quietly out onto the platform. He stepped up behind the demon, he could feel the cool night air and the wind rushing by him. The demon was standing next to the women, still whispering into her ear. Leahcim lunged forward and pushed the demon off the platform! He hit the ground and rolled down the embankment and crashed into the rocks at the bottom. Leahcim watched as the demon stood up, confused, and then fell backward into the river below. He turned to the women, she was still standing there near the edge, crying and looking at the river below. He leaned in and put his hand on her shoulder, and then whispered softly "God knows and cares... you'll be ok... everything will be ok."

A spirit of hope flooded the woman's heart. She stepped back from the edge, her eyes opened wide, and suddenly she smelled the cool night air. It smelled so fresh and invigorating! She felt the wind in her hair, and she thought of her husband...*he would want me to live,* she thought.

He would want me to laugh again and love again. He would want me to live...

Leahcim kissed her forehead and went back inside. He didn't know what to expect when he opened the door to the cabin, would Amy really have knocked out Johnathan's teeth? He wouldn't put it past her, she was a feisty one.

Instead of finding a brawl, the two were sitting opposite each other, both sitting straight up and staring at each other. Amy's eyes were wide, a single tear running down her cheek, she looked terrified. Leahcim stopped and sat the tray on the seat next to Johnathan.

"What's going on...," he started.

Then he heard a low growl. He turned, in the doorway of the bathroom there was an ugly little demon. He looked like a hairless dog, his ears back, and his teeth showing a constant line of drool coming from its mouth. It turned and looked at Leahcim, then he suddenly pounced on Leahcim, knocking him into the wall. The two fell on the seat next to Johnathan and rolled onto the floor, the demon was biting at Leahcim's face. Leahcim had its neck in his hands, holding him off, the demon was growling and snapping at Leahcim.

"Hit him!" Leahcim shouted.

Amy jumped across the two rolling on the floor and grabbed the food tray. The food went flying as she swung the tray, hitting Leahcim squarely across the face.

"OW! NOT ME, HIM!" This time she held the tray with both hands and swung with all her might, just as Leahcim pushed the demons head up and away from himself. She struck him hard across the forehead with the edge of the tray, his head split open and he fell back, slumping to the floor. A green slime began running from the demon's head, spilling out onto the floor.

"Eww gross," Amy said covering her nose with her sweater, "What's that smell!?"

"Rotting blood," Leahcim replied.

"Is it dead?" Johnathan asked.

"No, these don't die unless you cut their heads off. They just kind of drift off for a while, he'll regenerate in a few days."

"What do we do with it?"

"We'll hide him in the bathroom until the next stop, and then we'll get off this train. Hopefully the others won't come looking for him before then."

They wrapped the demon in a sheet and put him in the bathroom and closed the door. Leahcim soaked the slimy goo up off the floor with toilet paper and flushed it. The smell hung in the air.

The next stop was a small border town that the train barely slowed down for. The three jumped off the train as it slowed, right before it entered the station and disappeared into the dark.

CHAPTER 8
Miguel Lesous Perez

The three weary travelers were in a very small town in south Texas. They could see no name or identifying signs, but they found an abandoned gas station and slipped inside. As they moved around in the dark their eyes struggled to see anything at all. A car turned the corner outside and the headlights flashed through the windows of the gas station. Amy, Johnathan and Leahcim found themselves face to face with three very tough, fully tattooed, leather wearing, sweaty Mexican bikers.

Amy screamed, Johnathan screamed and Leahcim found himself nose to nose with the leader.

"Who are jou's?" The leader said in a very thick Mexican accent.

"You can see me!" Leahcim replied shocked.

"Jes, of course I can see jou."

"You shouldn't be able to see me!"

"Why? Do I look blind to jou?" He said angrily.

"No... um" Leahcim swallowed hard, "no not at all, it's just that...are you sure you can see me?" He stuttered, confused.

"I am standing here looking at jou, and those other two behind jou!" The biker said impatiently.

"I'm sorry, is he calling us Jews?" Johnathan asked.

"No I didn't say JEW, I clearly said JOU!"

"Because it sounds like you're saying Jew."

"I am saying jou, as in if JOU don't give me jour wallet, I'm going to choot JOU!"

"Now you're saying choo choo?"

"No! Not choo-choo, CHOOT JOU!" He yelled impatiently.

"I'm sorry, I'm not getting this." Johnathan said.

"Listen to my very clear English that I am speaking. If JOU DON'T GIVE ME JOR WALLETS, I'M GOING TO CHOOT ALL THREE OF JOU'S!"

"Wait, now you want to shoot three Jews?" Johnathan said, shaking his head in confusion.

"What? NO, ESSAY! What is it with jou and the Jews?" The leader said, "Jou have something against the Jews?"

"No, I like the Jews, they're fine people."

"Then why is it jou want me to kill three Jews?"

"I DIDN'T SAY THAT YOU SAID THAT! You said you were going to shoot you three Jews!!"

The leader straightened his back, bit his lip and said, "Jou listen to me, ok?" He continued,

"I am for the Jewish people. My people and their people are held together by Santa Maria Alaba a Dios!" He said as he crossed his chest.

"Oh, I know her!" Said Leahcim, "I've met her, wonderful woman!"

"Jou know the Mother? Jor telling me jou met the Holy Mother?! Ay ay ay elogair Dios!" He crossed himself again. "So jous don't hate the Jews, that is good, now I won't rob jou!"

"No, we never said we hated Jews you said....oh never mind, forget it!" Johnathan said.

"We are just trying to get to Jerusalem that's all"

"Jerusalem? So jou are Jews and jour going home to fight for jor freedom? A noble cause! Jou know, I am Jewish myself!" He smiled.

Johnathan shrugged his shoulders and looked at Amy as he shook his head in confusion.

"Now I understand," Miguel said. "Jou don't hear so good English. Problee because jou are Jewish and are used to jor own language. I will help jou, and interpret for jou ok? Don't worry."

"What?...No...," Johnathan said.

"We will join jou's and fight with jou's!" He said proudly. "I am Miguel Lesous Perez, and these is my gang."

"Your gang," Amy chirped raising her eyebrow, "all three of you?"

"Perez is Jewish?" Johnathan asked.

"Jess, Perez is a Jewish name. Jou think because of my good English, I can't be Jewish??"

"I just...," Johnathan started again, but gave up.

Leahcim said, "Miguel are you...," (He was going to ask if they had been sent by God to help but thought better of it.)

"What?"

"Never mind."

"So, when do we leave for Jerusalem?" Miguel asked.

"Well it's a bit complicated," Leahcim said. "We can't fly, so we have to get to New York somehow and catch a boat."

"No problem, we will take jou to New Jork on our bikes."

"That would be wonderful," Leahcim said. "How nice, a bike ride!"

"Jou guys look like jou could use some food. We will eat and get some sleep, then first thin in the morning leave for New Jork." He shouted across the room, " Chewy, some food for our Jewish amigos! Vaminos!"

"We're not...," Johnathan started to say and then gave up.

Johnathan and Amy were sitting next to Leahcim while the gang made dinner, which was deviled ham and stale bread.

Johnathan whispered to Leahcim, "How can they see us?"

"I'm not sure, I've heard other angels talk about seers, but I've never run across one before."

"What's a seer?" Amy asked.

"A human that can see angels and demons, very, very rare."

"Like a palm reader?"

"No, those are witches, most of them just see what they want, it's all in their heads. Although demons do show up and try to imitate dead people, you know loved ones and the like. No, seers just have this ability to see what they shouldn't be able to see. It usually doesn't last very long though."

The six of them ate their fill of the deviled ham and stale bread. Then they found the least smelly place to settle in and sleep for what was the rest of the night.

The next morning Johnathan was roused by the sound of Miguel and Leahcim laughing. They were all standing out in front of the gas station talking. Johnathan heard Leahcim say, "I'm so relieved you're here, Miguel."

Miguel put his hand on Leahcim's shoulder and said, "We'll make it, don't worry."

Amy sat up and stretched, hair covering her face, she grumbled, "I hate this." Amy and Johnathan stumbled outside to join the others.

"Good morning to jou sunchine!" Miguel said to Amy.

"Ugh," Amy said.

"Are jou guys ready to go?"

"No!" Amy said, "I need an espresso, makeup, clean clothes, and no voices for at least five hours!"

Miguel walked over to her and handed her a large espresso with whip, and two Splendas. Then he gave her a small makeup bag nestled on top of a set of clean, new clothes. He pointed to a chair beside the front door and said, "Please, take jor time, jest not five hours, ok?" Amy was shocked and said, "O....k." She scampered off to the chair.

Miguel turned to Johnathan and said, "Good morning my new Jewish friend, I am so glad to see jou!"

"I'm not..." Johnathan started and then stopped abruptly.

"I, Miguel, have also brought jou a set of clean clothes. With a nice new kippah. Have some coffee and a doughnut, and then we'll get out of here. Jor friend told me about the demons. Don't worry we have dealt with these pigs before, right amigos?" He looked at his gang, they all responded with smiles

"Kippah?" Johnathan said.

"Jess, for jour head, jou know, we are Jewish," he pointed back and forth to himself and Johnathan.

"I...," Johnathan just shook his head. "Do they ever talk?" Johnathan asked, pointing to Miguel's friends.

"No, they lost their tongues."

"Ow! How can you *lose* your tongue?"

"Nephilim."

"What's Nephilim?"

"Let's hope jou never find out, amigo. Go eat and drink, we will leave when jou wake up a little."

Leahcim stayed and talked with Miguel, Amy and Johnathan sat by the door drinking their coffees. Amy was smiling and sipping her expresso.

Johnathan said, "Don't you find this a little weird?"

"What?" Amy said.

"Miguel, and the coffee, the doughnuts, the makeup, the clothes, and a kippah? Where do you get a kippah? Where did it all come from?"

"I don't care. I love that smelly guy. I'm riding with *him*, you can have his chubby little friend."

His chubby little friends were Pedro and Chewy. Chewy being the chubby one, Pedro was tough, young, and basically fearless. Oh, and very lean with a good muscular build. Willing to fight at Miguel's prompting without question.

Chewy was a little fat guy who always carried with him an old brown distressed leather satchel. It had a long leather strap and a thousand zippered pockets where Chewy kept a plethora of snacks and bandages. He was the caregiver of the group, always ready to feed or bandage his

friends. They called him chewy because he was always chewing food of some kind. Both Chewy and Pedro were always smiling and eager to help anyone at any time, and loyal to Miguel to the death.

Johnathan got up and walked around the side of the building, drinking his coffee as he walked. He went back inside to find the restroom. As he made his way through the building he saw graffiti on one of the walls that in big blue letters said, HELL HOUNDERS.

"What's a hell hounder I wonder?" He said out loud. He made his way back out front and sat down next to Amy, as he looked over at her, he thought, *That's a hell hounder*! He smiled to himself. They sipped their coffees and ate doughnuts while Amy finished her makeup and went inside and changed. She returned happy as a lark, new clothes, makeup and plenty of insults at her ready.

"Are jou guys ready?" Miguel shouted.

Amy jumped up and said, "Yep, all set!"

Miquel led them around the side of the building. Amy noticed that the leather vests the three were wearing said HELL HOUNDERS, in large letters. Miguel handed Amy a helmet and said jou'll have to wear this." Amy stopped and giggled.

"What's being so funny?" Miguel asked.

"These are your bikes?" she said. "They are mopeds! You're a Mexican Moped gang!"

"Are we gonna knock off a Chuck-E-Cheese later? Now I understand the vests."

"Jou gotta charp tonque on jou, don't let looks fool jou, we are tougher than jou think!"

"I'm sure they shake in their little boots every time they see you coming," she giggled.

"Why can't we take that?" She pointed to an old VW van parked next to the building. It was painted with flowers and peace signs, and said *Make Tacos, Not War*! across it in big blue letters.

"Chure, we can take that. We used it back when we were feeding the hippies, but it still works."

The six gang members piled into the van and after a few attempts the old van popped, backfired, and blew out tons of black smoke. But it finally puttered back to life.

"We saved a lot of hippies in this old van," Miguel said. "Remember hombres?" The two smiled and gave the thumbs up.
Johnathan asked Miguel, "What does the Hell Hounders mean, on your jacket?"

"We fight those pigs, jou know, the hounds of hell."

"So you're angels?"

"No, we are not angels. We were created a little lower than the angels, but we've seen a lot of stuff most people can't see. And then when we find those pigs, we fight!" He said, eyes sparkling. "We gotta long ride ahead of us, we better git moving," Miguel said as he pulled the old van out onto the road. The old taco van bucked, puffed and popped again as he gave it gas. They puttered down the road, it was starting to get cloudy, and they saw lightning flash off in the distance. They were headed into a storm.

CHAPTER 9
The Sons of God

The demons arrived back at Walmart and were waiting in the room outside Lucifer's office. They still had the two demons that were tied and gagged and dressed as humans. They could hear Lucifer yelling at some poor demon through the door, and they were nervous. He was already in a bad mood it seemed. But they thought he would be very pleased that they had captured the two souls he requested.

When Lucifer gets angry, he has a hard time keeping his human form intact. He kind of fades in and out between his human form and his mist. When he changes back to his blackness, the demons know it's time to run!

He was yelling really loud... about a human. "I WANT HIM TO BEAT HIS WIFE AND THEN BEAT HER AGAIN AND AGAIN!" He was fading in and out of his mist. "IF HE'S NOT DRUNK, HE WONT BEAT HER," now he was all mist. "IF HE DOESN'T BEAT HER, SHE'LL GET HIM INTO REHAB, THEN INTO CHURCH AND THEN HE'S LOST FOREVER!"

He continued, now as his human form returned, "You steal the money and get it into his hands. Then you take him by his ear and get him to the liquor store! If he's not beating her by tonight, I'm going to let your idiot friends BEAT YOU INTO A GREEN MUSH! NOW GO!"

Lucifer was really angry, he was a black mist again, sitting behind his desk. The demons walked in slowly. Oh so cautiously, as all they could see was his hand as he began to turn back to his human form. His long fingernails were tapping the top of the desk. Slowly his arm appeared, and then out of the mist his body formed. Tapping his fingers with one hand, his chin in his other hand. His eyes were just solid black, they tended to stay dark longer than the rest of his body, he looked up as he took his gaze away from the floor.

"WHAT!" he yelled.

"We got 'em Sir."

"Got who, monkey boy?"

"The two undecideds from Techas, Sir."

"TEXAS, TEXAS, TEXAS! URRGH IDIOT! Where are they?"

"Right there," he pointed at the two dressed demons.

Lucifer walked over to the one wearing the hat and pushed it off his head. As he did, the spirit of confusion left the demons. Lucifer watched as it rose and left the room.

He turned and faced the Captain, fuming, his body didn't fade in and out this time, he went straight to his blackness. He flew across the room and engulfed the demon in his black fog, the demon grabbed at his own throat and began to suffocate. He began to sweat. Lucifer dragged him to the wall and threw him against it. Then threw him to the ground, the demon still clutching his throat and gasping for air. Lucifer, without turning, pointed at the ground and the other demons went to their knees grasping their throats and struggling for air.

"YOU COMPLETE MORON! YOU PATHETIC EXCUSE OF A DEMON! A SPIRIT OF CONFUSION... REALLY?"

Lucifer let go of the Captain and released the others, they all fell to the ground gasping for air.

Lucifer remained as a thick black mist, breathing heavily. The dark cloud moved back and forth across the room, moving quickly as he thought. Back and forth... his legs and feet began to appear first, hooved feet, stomping across the floor. Then his legs, like that of a horse, now half mist and half body, stomping back and forth across the floor. The floor cracked as he stomped... the demons did not dare look up. They all remained curled up in balls, huddling on the floor, covering their ears.

He moved faster and faster stomping back and forth, his desk and the chairs began to hover. Things from the shelves began to float, then they all started crashing against the walls as he became angrier and angrier. Everything inside his office was being picked up and smashed against the walls, and against the demons - cutting them and breaking their bones. He threw the demons across the room, crashing them into bookshelves and tables. There was a great sound, like that of a rushing tornado, glass and pieces of broken furniture were flying around the room... Suddenly... everything stopped. Silence.

Lucifer's thick black cloud was just hanging in midair, it seemed to be trembling in the air.

"NEPHILIM!" He screamed.

He picked up the Captain by his throat and said, "Nephilim."

"Please, lord no!"

"GET ME THE SONS OF GOD!"

"I beg you, please, Sir...please, send one of the others to get them."

The Son's of God were the 'mighty men of old', they are the oldest warriors known. They are fierce fighters, and *terrifying* demons. As angels, they revolted against God with Lucifer, and were cast to earth with him. Lucifer made them his warriors, ready to fight God and His army in the end battle to come. In the meantime he gave them free reign, and left them to their own mayhem.

Since the fall, these demons have been left unchecked by Lucifer, with no intervention or influence. They went out of control, wreaking havoc and doing whatever they pleased. They even went as far as to take on human form and have sex with human women, which created giant men, who became known as the Sons of Anak. This angered God mightily, and they were a big part of God's decision to 'start over'. Some were imprisoned by God, but most of these mighty men of old were 'destroyed' in the flood. However, the ones that were killed in the flood then became disembodied spirits, and still roam about.

These Nephilim were a force even Lucifer dreaded. They answered to no one, not even Lucifer. They were their own driving force, because they thoroughly enjoyed evil acts, and all the torment they could create. Although, over the centuries, they have been a great asset to Lucifer. They have been the driving force in the mass killings of millions and millions of people, throughout history. From Tomas de Torquemada and Mao Zedong, to Hitler and Stalin. The genocide in Rwanda, the killing fields of Cambodia, to the terrorists of today, all their leaders were influenced by these demons, and they are very proud of their work.

To call out these demons meant that there was something going on that the other demons didn't get, something big.

"Why the Sons of God, Lord? We can get them, we don't need those guys."

Lucifer was back in his body still pacing, "See if you can keep up on this ok? If you were duped by a spirit of confusion, that means there's an angel here. If there's an angel here, that means he's stuck here. If he's stuck here, then that means he has no protection here. No protection means all bets are off, and I can do anything I want with all of them."

The demon looked confused.

"I'm going to beat you to death with a puppy," he said shaking his head. He continued, "He has no protection, maybe a few stones to throw at you morons, but nothing he can use against me. I can capture an angel, actually catch one of those burrs in my butt, and hold him for ransom."

"For a million dollars!" The demon said it, and instantly regretted it.

"Go get me a puppy! Go on, right now! Get the hell out of here and go find the Sons of God and bring them here!"

"What about the two undecideds?"

"They can rot in the field, I don't care about them."

"Can I have them?"

"Why, what for?"

"Practice, you know... torture... I liked your idea of the whole puppy thing."

"Whatever."

Lucifer put his office back together and sat down, *Who is this stupid little angel? It's gotta be a trainee. You messed up little man, whoever you are. I need to find a place to stash this puke,* he thought, *Where? Where do you hide an angel from God? Where's the one place he can't see or won't look...*

Lucifer still believed he was going to win this war, he still believed that he could take God's place on the throne and rule heaven. "Having an angel might be better than a human," he said out loud. "Imagine if I could turn this angel to my side... *Oh the secrets he must know...He thought. It's been a long time since the fall, and things probably changed when God shot me to the ground in a lightning bolt! This angel might be able to tell me things only the white ones know. Maybe he's fully empowered! That kind of power in the hands of a dark one!*

This could change the whole course of things. Maybe he could control death, oh, he thought, *that would be awesome! I'd kill every one of those apes! Wipe out God's plan with one blow! Oh, but they would suffer first, such agonizing deaths, all while God watched. This is so awesome,* he thought, *I'm so excited, I haven't been this excited since that little wench ate the apple!* "My own white one... an angel that didn't suffer the fall. The possibilities are endless!" He said to the empty room.

CHAPTER 10
Good Enough

As they drove it became very dark, the clouds were beginning to build. A storm was coming, lightning flashed from the sky, then the rain came down in sheets. As Miguel drove, fighting to see through the old cracked windshield, the wipers were barely able to keep up with the rain. Johnathan looked at Miguel and began questioning him.

"So how is it that you can see us?"

Leahcim looked at Johnathan and shook his head, "no" he mouthed.

"We are not so different from jou, except we're alive and jor dead... sort of. I too was once dead." Miguel said.

"Really?"

"Jes I was, for three days."

"Three days!" Johnathan said it, knowing it was impossible, he thought *ok this guy is a nut case!* "Please tell."

"Well," Miguel started, "it was a very long time ago, I was much younger. All I can tell jou is that when I woke up, I could see things I couldn't see before. These pigs that we fight, the ones chasing jou, they are everywhere. They never sleep, they never eat, and the really bad ones are the ones who cut out my amigo's tongues."

"So you can see us, and you can see the demons too."

"Jes, both."

"Well, do you know why he can't get a hold of anyone in heaven?" He asked, pointing to Leahcim. "I mean have you ever seen anything like this before?"

"No, this I have not seen before. But I have seen demons try to look like the dead, jou know, like someone's mother or husband, but they can't do it for very long, it drains them. Not even Lucifer can keep that one going."

Just then a man darted out in front of the van, he was running as fast as he could across the road. Miguel slammed on the brakes just as a demon slammed into the front of the van. He put his hands on the glass and looked through the window. It snarled, showing its teeth and growled, and then it turned and ran after the man. Suddenly three more men ran across the road, carrying baseball bats, followed by two more demons running and panting after them.

Miguel yelled "Hombres vamonos!"

The three jumped from the van and ran into the woods after the demons.

Amy, Johnathan and Leahcim followed a short distance behind. When they caught up to the group, Miguel and his two friends had the demons pinned up against an outcropping of rocks. Miguel walked up to them and said something that the three could not hear, when he did, the demons put their hands up as if covering their faces and slid back against the wall keeping as far away from Miguel as possible. Then they ran off into the wilderness. Miguel turned to the three men who were now surrounding the terrified man, the rain was pouring down as lightning lit the sky above them.

"FAGGOT!" One man shouted.

"GOD HATES FAGGOTS YOU QUEER!" Said another as he raised his bat.

"WHO SAID?" Miguel shouted.

The three turned to face this intruder. "Who said God hates gay men?" Miguel asked again.

"Did He tell jou this? Did He say 'I hate gay men' to jou personally? Because He never said this thing to me."

"Who the hell are you?"

"I am, just...me Miquel Lesous Perez"

"A DAMN MEXICAN! That's who you are! God ain't too happy with you either! Why don't you swim back across the border where you belong, boy?"

One of the other men started yelling, "I'll tell you who said it, Beaner! God said it in the bible! He hates fags!"

"Jou are mistaken, my friend. He said He hates the act, never the actor, the actor He loves.
But do jou know what else He hates? He hates the *hate* in jor hearts," he turned to the first man, "and He hates it when jou get drunk and beat jor wife, and then go to church and sing praise.
And do jou know what else He hates?" He turned to the second man, "He hates it when jou abuse and shame your own children, and then drag them off to church."
Turning to the last one, "He hates it when jou leave bruises on jour mothers arm because jou want to drink more than jou want to help her. And then... take her to church on Sunday.
He hates the *hate* in jor hearts, but he does not hate the haters."

Miguel continued, "Let me ask jou this, which death is worse? If jou kill this man, or kill his hope of salvation? If jou stand in front of jor Father and say, "Look, we killed this gay man for jor name's sake," and the Father say's to jou, "But tomorrow he would have heard the truth, and turned to me. And now jou have robbed him of his chance to come to me, because he will never know. Whose death is worse, his or jors?"

The three men looked at each other, soaking wet they began to leave. One by one they put down their bats and turned, disappearing into the woods.

Miguel walked over to the man standing in the rain, wet and scared, he put his arm around him and said, "Let's get jou home my friend."

They made their way back through the woods to the van. As they drove, Leahcim prayed silently. Amy and Johnathan sat in silence looking out the windows at the rain. They both held what Miguel had said, in their hearts, and did not speak. After a short drive they had the man back to his home. Before he got out, Miguel said to him, "Don't judge God by the acts of ignorant men. These tree tonight do *not* represent jor Father in heaven. If jou ask Him to cho jou the truth, He will. Go in peace my friend." The man left the van and headed into his home.

They drove away into the rain, back to the highway heading south. Just as the sun began to set, Amy saw the sign 'Welcome To Louisiana'. Miguel looked in the mirror at Leahcim as they watched the sign go by, Leahcim raised his eyebrows and sighed.

They drove on for a few hours, and eventually Miguel decided they should stop for food and a place to sleep for the night. He pulled into a small town and found a small motel with a café. A large neon sign read 'Hello Café and Motel'. The O in hello kept blinking in and out as the bulb was burning out. As they entered the café the O exploded and sparked, and finally burnt out.

As Miguel ordered enough dinner for him, his companions, and Amy and Johnathan, they began to talk about demons and what Amy and Johnathan should expect.

Leahcim began, "Listen, there are some things you should know about these demons."

"Ok" Johnathan said.

" You must understand that our struggle is not against flesh and blood, but against the rulers, against the authorities, against the powers of this dark world and against the spiritual forces of evil in the haevenly realms." Leahcim continued, "Most of these are whisperers or gatherers. All of them believe in God and tremble at His name. They're not afraid of you, but they are afraid of God."

"What about Lucifer, is he afraid of God?" Amy asked.

"No, when you have nothing to lose you tend to lose all fear. He is the accuser now, and he only fears losing this war."

"Who is he accusing, and of what?" Johnathan asked.

"He's accusing you and her, and everyone God ever created. He accuses you of all your faults, of everything you've ever done, and he brings these accusations in front of God and demands your soul. If you're a non-believer, the accusations stick, and the case is closed, and you're whisked away in chains and separated from God. But in the cases of believers, these accusations although true as they are, and they *are* true... God turns to the defense table and waits for 4 words..."

"What words?" Amy asked.

"This one is mine," Miguel said.

"That's right," Leahcim replied.

"Lucifer can't overcome the cross. Believers still, and always will, offend... but the cross... the Son... erased all of that... past, present and future. It's like it never happened. You two being undecided, technically fall into the non-believer category. But since I missed the bell and the message I was to give, I think we have a chance of saving you two. I mean, technically... this time we're in right now... doesn't exist..., I think."

Johnathan said, "What if we believe now? I mean I'm convinced! I've seen enough! I have no doubt God is real!"

"So do the demons," replied Miguel. "They believe too," he continued.

Leahcim said, "I'm not sure what the outcome of this will be. Right now we have to concentrate on getting to Jerusalem alive. But we have to believe there is a plan, or a contingency of some kind. That means staying away from dark ones, we may have a bigger problem than just the everyday demons," Leahcim said.

"Johnathan," Amy said.

"No, not Johnathan."

Johnathan shot Amy a dirty look.

"We were talking this morning," he motioned to Miguel, "If time doesn't exist right now, if it's in suspension while heaven is closed, then it could mean that I'm fair game too. What I mean is, Lucifer may see this as an opportunity to capture me as well. If he figures this out, he will stop at nothing to get me, I would be a bigger prize than the two of you."

"What if we give them Amy, and we make our get away?" Johnathan said.

"We'd have to," Amy said. "I'm sure they're looking for sharp minds not goat cheese."

"Listen," Leahcim said, "We think Lucifer will eventually call in the Nephilim, and that's not a good thing."

"Nephilim?" Johnathan said. "You said something about them earlier, what are they?"

"The Nephilim are fallen angels as well. They are also called 'The Mighty Men of Old' or 'The Sons of God', so if you hear me refer to them that way, you'll know. The difference with these fallen angels is that when God wiped them out in the flood a lot of them actually died. Remember when you asked if we could kill demons?"

"Yes"

"Well the problem is, you don't want to kill them because then they become disembodied spirits. And disembodied spirits need a place to go... and that's when you get possessions, spirits taking over humans. They're very hard to spot and extremely dangerous, they have superhuman strength and they're almost impossible to expel."

"Well, how will we know if they're here?"

"Black eyes," Miguel said. "Have jou ever seen a person and when jou look at them their eyes are just black? But then jou see them again and they're blue or brown?"

"Yea, my landlord, he has those eyes sometimes."

"Well what jou're seeing is the Nephilim inside him. They move from person to person that's why sometimes his eyes are blue but then black, the spirit moves in and out of them."

"Well, can we kill them?'

"Jou can't kill them. Jou can kill the host body, but the demon will just move on."

"Lucifer has to find them first. He lost track of them when they were disembodied. He sees their handy work, and they're his trusted servants because they do such a good job. But they're also hard to find. So now," Leahcim said, "we have to watch out for humans as well. If they show up, we'll start seeing humans coming after us. If we're in a crowd they can jump from one human to another, to another before we even know they're there. Just be sure you stay close to me from now on, arm's length ok?"

"Ok," Johnathan replied.

"Amy?"

"Yea ok," she said. Amy looked around the café and wondered who in the crowd could be one of them.

"Let's get a room and hide out til morning." Miguel said.

They checked into one of the rooms at the end of the motel near the road. Amy said, "Oh thank someone there's a shower!" She headed for the bathroom as Johnathan flopped onto one of the beds.

"Jou guys stay in here with Leahcim. We'll stay in the van and keep guard, if jou need us we'll be right outside." Miguel and his companions left the room, leaving the three alone for the night.

"Why doesn't God just let everyone into heaven, I mean the good ones?" Johnathan asked.

"Where's the line?" Leahcim said.

"What do you mean?'

"Well, if everyone who is good gets into heaven, then there must be by definition, a line of some kind. A boundary line that if you cross it, then it's not 'good enough'. Is it stealing?"

"Well no... stealing shouldn't keep you from heaven," Johnathan answered.

"Ok, how about rape? Or murder?"

"Yea, rape and murder you should definitely go to hell."

"Ok," Leahcim said. "What about cheating on your wife, or beating your children? Or incest?"

"I guess those too."

"What about drugs? And how about lying, or greed? What about the guy who lies to his boss to get someone's job, destroying the other man's life and putting him and his family on the street? Should he be in heaven?" Leahcim continued, "If everyone went to heaven that was as you put it, 'good enough'... then essentially...you're in heaven now. Take away the 'bad ones', and poof this is heaven! You would still have, jealousy, envy, greed, lying, stealing, child abuse, drug abuse and so on. Not very nice, is it?"

"So, what's the answer?" Johnathan asked.

"Make a bridge."

"A bridge?" Johnathan said.

"Yes, a bridge from all of this ugliness to God. He wants everyone."

"You lost me," Johnathan said shaking his head.

"God is a just God, a kind God, a merciful God, and infinitely patient with you. He is full of grace and mercy." Leahcim said, with a soft loving tone in his voice. "He made a way for **all** to enter the kingdom of heaven, and it's as simple as faith in his Son. Nothing else." Leahcim took a deep breath and said, "There's something wonderful and powerful about admitting all you've done against God and man. Telling him everything, holding nothing back... on your knees saying "forgive me" in front of the most powerful being in all creation. The thing is, He already *knows* what you're going to admit, it's not like He's going to be shocked or surprised. You humans seem to think He can't see you until you talk to him. But He's there, He's always there." Leahcim looked at Johnathan. "The transformation that takes place in a man or woman or child is the most amazing thing to watch. That old person who lied, cheated, murdered, is forgiven and then they change...I have to tell you Johnathan, sometimes I don't understand it myself, but I've seen it with my own eyes."

Johnathan was listening intently.

"Johnathan I've seen men who have been possessed by Nephilim at one time, come to God. It's all about the heart Johnathan, always the heart."

"Everyone." Johnathan said.

"Yes, everyone."

Just then Amy came out of the bathroom drying her hair with a towel. Johnathan looked at Leahcim...

"Everyone." Leahcim said. Amy smiled at Leahcim and looked at Johnathan and said, "Pig!"

CHAPTER 11
Dogs

The Captain of Lucifer's army went about searching out the Nephilim. Finding something that can't be seen is a difficult task. *Death*, he thought, *where is there lots and lots of death these days?...TERRORISTS! We're going to Iraq! Where though?* He thought himself to a mosque where he used to work, whispering to the worshipers, before he was promoted to Captain.

He slammed into the side of the mosque and his assistant hit the top of the cab parked in front. They dusted themselves off and began to run towards the Syrian border, noses in the air as they ran, sniffing for the scent of death, they moved quickly. As they ran across the sand, the Captain caught the scent of blood. He stopped and looked, turning in circles following the scent. He moved from one direction to the other his nose now to the ground... the scent was getting stronger. He moved over a sand dune, his breath kicking up the sand as he sniffed, and he stopped at a pool of red sand. Blood! He looked up and sniffed the air, "We're close," he said. "The blood of a human... They're here."

In the distance they could see a small town, the two headed down the sand dune and into the town. The town was full of dark ones, whisperers were everywhere. He approached a young man dressed in black, a whisperer was standing behind him saying "Infidels! Pigs! Shoot every one of them in the head! Allah will be pleased with this!"

The Captain took the demon by his throat, "Nephilim. Lucifer wants the Nephilim."

The demon pointed to a building in the center of town, and he dropped the demon. The two walked to the building and went inside.

It was dark inside, the room was filled with men in black uniforms, sitting at tables and standing in small groups. There were no dark ones that he could see, but there was a darkness that the Captain found refreshing, it felt warm to him. He looked around the room, everyone was busy planning. They had maps and laptops, pictures of American, French, German, and British landmarks that were posted all over the walls.

The Captain walked over to the first man that he saw, his eyes were pitch black.

"What?" the demon inside him screamed "What do you want from us?!?"

"Lucifer is looking for you."

"Why?"

"He needs your help."

"WE'RE BUSY HERE!" His head was listing to the side almost resting on its shoulder.

"There's a white one trapped on earth... he wants to capture it."

The body the demon was using began to struggle, jumping and twitching, the mans eyes turned brown as he regained his body. The demon flew across the room and slammed into the body of another soldier, it was a violent occurrence, as the man gave into the possession and his eyes turned black.

The demon shouted at the Captain from across the room, "We can kill *hundreds* here *every* day, why give that up for one white one!?"

"Lucifer wants to hold it for ransom."

"Hold a white one hostage from GOD?" The demon stepped back and leaned against the wall, the body he was in began to struggle. He yelled "ARRGG! STOP IT!" as he slammed the body into the wall.

He walked towards the Captain, "Every single human in this room and a hundred rooms like it all across this country will be blown up or shot or hung! All thanks to us! Lucifer had nothing to do with this!"

"What's your point demon?" the Captain asked.

"WE WANT BODIES!"

"You have any body you want now!"

"WE WANT OUR OWN BODIES, THE BODY WE USED TO HAVE BEFORE HE DESTROYED THEM... BEFORE THE FLOOD!"

The body he was in collapsed onto the floor it began to shake and foam at the mouth. The demon left it and circled the building flying high against the ceiling, he circled the room groaning as he flew. The door opened as a soldier entered, and the demon dove at the door and hit the soldier knocking him into a table and onto the floor.

"We want bodies as part of the ransom!" He said as he picked himself up.

"Why would Lucifer demand bodies for you?"

As he was speaking another demon in the room stood up and yelled, "ALLAHU AKBAR."

As he did the entire room followed the man outside. The crowd made their way down an alley and into a large courtyard, and there in the center was a woman tied to a pole on her knees. She was covered with a blanket and had been badly beaten. Her chains were just long enough for her to cover her nakedness with the thin cloth, she was crying, and begging for mercy.

As they arrived many people from the town joined their mob, whisperers were feeding the frenzy, and the mob grew in size. The whisperers were moving through the crowd saying, "STONE HER, STONE HER, SHE'S A WHORE! STONE HER!"

The crowd was worked into a frenzy, and the demons were running from person to person chanting. The man possessed by the demon began to fight violently with the demon, trying desperately to free himself, but the demon resisted all the more. It was *his* wife tied to the pole.

The demon began to speak, "This WHORE was caught in the act of adultery! By Allah's law, she must be stoned! She must pay for her sin with her life, for the honor of her husband!"

The crowd all picked up rocks and bricks and anything they could find to throw at the woman. The demon turned and faced the woman, holding a large rock in his hand he threw his stone striking her in the face. The crowd joined in, throwing rocks and bricks, the sound of her screams filled the air... the stones hitting their mark time and time again, breaking her bones, and tearing her skin. The demons were dancing and skipping in a circle around the woman's dying body, laughing as they danced.

The Captain looked at the possessed man, as the demon left his body the man slumped to his knees and wept. The other demon jumped into another man in the crowd, then turned to the Captain and said, "That's why Captain! Would you like to see a beheading?"

The Captain smiled and said, "I think Lucifer will agree."

"Where does he want us?" The demon asked.

"Louisiana."

"When?"

"As soon as we locate the white one. Send one of your demons for now, and he can contact you once we find them."

"Done!" The demon replied.

Lucifer was hanging from the ceiling, a noose wrapped tightly around his neck, dangling in the air and swinging back and forth. *I love this,* he thought, *suicide is such a wonderful way to go.*
He heard something slam into his office door. He rolled his eyes, "One of the idiots has blundered home," he said under his breath.

The door opened, it was the Captain.

"Found em, Lord!"

A cold presence followed the Captain into the room, the air was chilled, and it surrounded the demon.

"I need a body!" The demon demanded.

"Lure someone back here from the store," he motioned to the Captain.

As they waited Lucifer walked around the presence, circling it, examining it. "Cold?" He asked.

"Always cold," it replied.

"You'll be warm in a minute."

"We want bodies for the exchange."

"What exchange?"

"The ransom you're going to get from God, for the white one. We want permanent bodies. We've been cold for four thousand years! Your Captain agreed!"

"My Captain is an idiot. Besides, if you had bodies, you would have no motivation to possess. No motivation means no death and mayhem, so why would I agree to bodies?"

"We won't help unless you agree."

"A strike! You're going to strike? How about I cast you into the lake of fire and watch you burn for eternity? Still wanna negotiate?"

"Sounds nice actually, we'd be warm finally after four thousand years of ICE! We followed you Lucifer, you promised we would rule with you! And what did we get for our rebellion? Cast into darkness with no light, no warmth, NO BODIES! We're sick of being cold, and we're sick of jumping into these morons!! If we don't get bodies, you don't get a white one, and we will SEE TO THAT!!"

"DON'T YOU FORGET WHO YOU SERVE DEMON!" Lucifer shouted at him as he began to fade to his blackness.

"We serve NO ONE Lucifer! You can't control us anymore! I swear to you Morning Star, we will wreak havoc UNLIKE ANYTHING YOU AND YOUR PATHETIC DOGS HAVE *EVER* WITNESSED – AND IT WON'T BE AGAINST HUMANS THIS TIME – WE WILL COME AGAINST YOU!!!!" He roared.

Lucifer was all black, a cloud swaying back and forth. He fell silent, only the sound of his breath was heard, almost panting, staring at the demon's presence, the two didn't move, both hovering...

The door opened, and the Captain entered.

The Nephilim and Lucifer both turned and roared sending the Captain through the wall and into the hall outside. He rolled down an isle and crashed into a display, knocking a woman over. As she laid sprawled out on the floor next to the Captain, the Nephilim screeched as he flew across the room, thru the wall, and into the women on the floor. She jumped to her feet and began kicking the Captain, as hard as she could, in the head. She was fast and powerful, each blow stunning the Captain. She kept kicking and kicking until his head began to split. Green mush began to run from his head, he started twitching and convulsing, he tried to cover his head, but she was too fast and too strong. He curled into a fetal position and finally gasped his last breath, laying limp on the floor.

The Nephilim turned to Lucifer, "BODIES, MORNING STAR!!" She said, gulping to catch her breath, "OR WE'LL KILL EVERY DOG IN YOUR FOLD!"

CHAPTER 12
He Can't Sustain This

"Shower, pig!" Amy said to Johnathan. "Or don't trailer turds bathe? Can't get wet?"

"I don't believe in abortion Amy, but I think your mother should have thought that one through." He replied.

Leahcim smiled, "Love is so awesome, such a powerful force!"

"Love?" Amy said.

"Yea, you two, you're headed for love. I've seen it for thousands of years and it's such a wonderful thing to watch. Never gets boring to see!"

"Have you lost your mind!? Me and it? Never!" She quipped.

"Not gonna happen," Johnathan shivered and headed for the shower.

Amy laid down on the bed furthest from the window, pulling the blankets over her head and in a muffled voice said, "Goodnight, tooth fairy."

"Good night, my dear," he replied.

Amy drifted off into a deep sleep. She began to dream she was walking in a field full of flowers, they were up to her hips, and she ran them through her fingers as she walked. In the distance she heard a faint barking, a dog, she kept running the flowers through her fingers. The barking was getting closer... it was right behind her now... suddenly she was running! Faster and faster, her heart was pounding in her chest, and she kept looking behind her as she ran. The barking was right behind her, at her heels, she turned to see a large German shepherd snapping at her, drool coming from its mouth. Now as she turned back around she was in an alley... running as fast as she could... the dog turned the corner to the alley, he was coming! She could feel her heart beating faster, she tried to scream but nothing would come out! She jumped onto the fence at the end of the ally, the dog jumping up at her snapping it's sharp teeth at her feet.

Suddenly she was hanging from a ledge by her fingertips, she was in a large room made of concrete, and the room was filling with water. It was filling up fast, and the dog was still there swimming towards her and barking. She was hanging on as tight as she could, the dog was getting closer and closer... as the water rose the dog turned into a man... suddenly he was sitting on top of the ledge touching her fingers. He was facing away from her, his hand touching hers, she couldn't see his face.

"You can't hang on forever," he said. "Just let go, I'll catch you, you'll be safe with me."

The dog was back, swimming and barking as the water rose. Her heart was pounding as the dog got closer. She struggled to keep her grip, she looked at the dog and then back at the man, he turned his head toward her. His face was pale, long pointed nose and rotting sharp teeth. He had limbs protruding from his back that dripped with red and green pus that smelled of rotting flesh, his hands were boney and cold.

"Take my hand, I'll save you."

"Amy..." A small voice called, it seemed as though it were miles away.

"TAKE MY HAND!" The man said again, bolder this time.

"Amy...AMY....AMY LOOK AT ME!" The voice was getting louder. She turned her head, it was Leahcim standing in the water next to the dog. As he began to speak the dog sank under the water.

"AMY LOOK AT ME! HE CAN'T SUSTAIN THIS, IT'S LUCIFER, AMY. HE'S TRICKING YOU, LOOK AT ME!"

Amy sat straight up in the bed gasping for air.

"Amy," Leahcim said, "You're ok. It's ok, look at me...there that's better."

"Oh my god, what was that?" her heart was still racing.

"Lucifer," Leahcim replied. "He found his way into your dreams, it's just an illusion. He can't keep it up for very long. It's ok you're safe now! If he comes back again just start repeating **God is my defender, I will not be moved**! Over and over, keep saying it and he'll get frustrated and leave, ok?"

"Ok," she said, voice trembling.

"He can get in our dreams?" Johnathan asked.

"He can and will. It's good he's in her dreams though, it means he doesn't know where we are yet."

"That scared the crap out of me," Amy said.

"What would have happened if I took his hand?" she asked.

"Nothing really, it's more a psychological game than anything. You would have questioned your own loyalties in the end, it would just mess with your mind forever. Remember he's very good at this game, he's been playing it for thousands of years... but so have we."

Leahcim knew the meaning of the water in her dream but held it to himself for now.

Amy went to the window and opened the drapes, she could just make out the slightest hint of dawn breaking on the horizon. *Thank God!*, she thought.

Miguel and his companions looked refreshed, as if they had all had a great nights sleep. They were freshly showered and ready to go. Chewy started handing out fresh coffee and doughnuts, smiling and eager to start the day.

"Jou guys look terrible," Miguel said.

"Lucifer showed up in her dream last night," Leahcim replied.

"Well, it's better than in person!" Miguel said.

"Did you guys see anything?"

"No, it was quiet all the way to morning... except for Pedro and his deviled ham problem! Woo!!" He said waving at his nose.

Pedro blushed and grinned.

"Jou know, I have been thinking about dis trip we are on, if we drive to New Jork and then we take a boat to Europe, and then a train to France, and then we walk about ten thousand miles to Jerusalem we might make it by the time I die! No, I think we chood rethink our plan amigo."

"What do you suggest?" Leahcim asked.

"Well if we get to a plane before the Nephilim find us, I think we could clear the plane of demons before we take off. Then we fly as far as we can, maybe even all the way to the Holy Land." He said, as he crossed himself.

They planned the trip and decided that Leahcim could use one of his stones to fool the flight staff into thinking that Miguel and his friends were actually boxes of freight. Then they would fly in the cargo hold of a FedEx or another freight carrier. The six set out for the airport in Alexandria. They were about 3 hours from the airport, a small trip that would last days.

CHAPTER 13
The Son of A Motherless Goat

Lucifer was standing in the corner of his office, still in mist form, hovering in the corner facing the wall. His head was looking up at the ceiling, eyes closed arms stretched out.

"There you are, you little witch." He had found Amy in a dream. "Oh I know you," he said under his breath, "You're that rich little snot with the wonderfully bad attitude." He entered as a hound and began chasing her. She was caught off guard, he loved this, terrifying humans in their dreams! She started running across the field, her quiet peaceful place was now a place of torment. He caught up to her and began nipping at her heels, she ran faster... he turned the field into an alley with no way out. He let her get ahead of him, she was in a panic now, he could feel her heart pounding... she jumped up on the fence at the end of the alley, he jumped snapping at her feet, he turned the fence into a ledge and hung her there by her fingertips... her heart was beating so fast! He could feel the terror in her chest. He laughed to himself.

Suddenly a voice...very small, said, "Amy...Amy...," Lucifer looked up, someone else was there! *Who is this chubby puke? That's him! The angel! I don't recognize this one!* He thought. *The water! The Holy Spirit! NO!* He turned to Amy, he could feel his power fading, he reached out and tried to take her hand. His eyes glued to Leahcim, he didn't recognize him at all! If she would take his hand, he could at least confuse her. The angel was moving closer to her, "He can't sustain this...," the angel was telling her. He lost her, she was gone.

Lucifer dropped to the floor in his office, *UUGGGH!* He turned to the Nephilim still standing over the Captain's body. "FINE, YOU SON OF A MOTHERLESS GOAT! BODIES!" Lucifer bellowed. "You can have bodies, but I need to find them. I need to know what the hell they're planning, where they're going, and how they're getting there. All the details!! And I need them before heaven figures out that I know he's here alone!"

"Don't lie to us again Lucifer!"

"I'll demand bodies." He thought it best not to mention the Holy Spirit.

With that the Nephilim left Lucifer. He traveled back to Syria and gathered the demons, *twenty should do it, they've taken down entire nations with less*, he thought. Armed with twenty disembodied demons, they headed out to find the white one.

Azazel their leader, was known as the 'Demon of War'. He was very good at his craft, he was the first fallen angel who had taken on human form and had sex with human women. His children were huge men, great warriors that were called The Sons of Anak.

This act had angered God so greatly and He had decided to wipe them out and start over. So most of the Nephilim were killed in the great flood and became disembodied, some were imprisoned by God, some managed to escape. All of which only increased Azazel's hatred for humans, and of God! Although, he regretted the alliance he had made with Lucifer, and wished he had never joined the rebellion against God. Being cast into outer darkness was cold and hopeless. When they escaped the imprisonment and made their way back to earth, they found the only way to get warm and escape the freezing cold, was to possess humans. However, this was a temporary solution. They found they couldn't occupy a body very long, as the host would eventually get too uncomfortable and start fighting them, and they would have to jump to another human. Or if the cold became too unbearable they would use animals, but animals were very unpredictable and hard to control.

The human mind was much easier to influence, they had desires that animals didn't, like drinking, drugs or sex, and it was very easy to tap into their natural tendency for self-gratification, almost instantly. Getting a human to murder another human was not hard to do either, mass murder like with the Germans or Stalin was Azazel's forte.

As with all humans the key is pride and ego. Humans want to feel relevant and important, they thrive on anything that feeds those emotions. What Azazel had perfected was the ability to feed that very thing. Death he found, was a very powerful tool, get a human to kill once and killing 100,000 becomes an ego feeding frenzy. Convince them they have the power over life and death and they can become unstoppable, add money, fame, and terror... these were the tools of his trade.

Now, to find an angel and two humans, or near humans, shouldn't be that difficult a task. Capturing one was a different story as it had never been done. *How strong is he?* Azazel wondered. *Why can't he fly? Where is he taking them? And why can't God see them? There's something not right about this.* He thought. *It seems like a trap, but who's setting it? Lucifer or God? Is this angel bait, or a mistake?* He knew trials happen and that heaven would shut down on occasion, but God always kept it under control, and very tightly monitored. *The key,* he thought, *is in the staircase, how does an angel fall off the platform and onto earth?! Unless this angel is the dumbest one ever created... no this has to be a trap of some kind and it has to do with these two humans for some reason.* Lucifer wanted the angel for a ransom tool, but Azazel had a feeling the humans were at the center of this soup.

A body was very enticing, almost too good to be true. Four thousand years is a long time to be cold, but cast back out into outer darkness, or even worse imprisoned for eternity would definitely be worse. At least in his current form he could get warm from time to time and killing all these humans was just fun. He decided to play along with Lucifer for the time being and watch carefully for the trap that had most certainly been set. *Who knows, there may be an opportunity to overthrow Lucifer!* He thought.

Their spirits traveled quickly to the area the three were last seen, and they picked up some gatherers to help sniff out the group. They set the dogs on the ground, near the church, and started there. The hounds picked up the scent and they started out after them. The spirits riding on the backs of the gatherers, hitting them and digging their heels into the demon's sides until they howled in pain, making them move faster and faster. It wasn't long before they were in the room where the junkie was lying, his body cold and blue.

Azazel entered the man's body, it sat up, eyes grey with death, and blue lips... "ARGGG! COLD!" the young man's mouth said. He left the body and got back on his demon.

"They were here, keep looking!"

They left the building following the scent down the street, the demons howling in pain as they ran. The thrift store was filled with the scent, this was where the demons were fooled by Leahcim. Azazel found the used stone behind the counter, *angel's tricks,* he thought. The hounds picked up Amy's strong scent, and from there they ended up at the café, then on to the train station, and there the scent went cold.

"They must have caught a train," Azazel said. "Call in more Gatherers! Send fifty north and fifty south, find out if any have seen these three anywhere! Tell them there will be a promotion for anyone who comes forward!"

As they waited, a train pulled into the station, it rolled past and came to a stop. One of the gatherers put his nose in the air, he had caught the scent of something... not of the three, but of a gatherer... of split skin, and rotting flesh. It leapt onto the train, ran up and down the aisles nose in the air. He stopped at a cabin, and burst through the door, sniffing from side to side. He went into the bathroom, and there in the shower stall, he found the whisperer that Amy had smashed in the head. He was almost back together, head still oozing green pus. He dragged the still wounded demon out onto the platform and threw him on the ground in front of Azazel. It hit the ground with a thud, and a groan.

"This was in a cabin," the gatherer said.

Azazel grabbed the demon by the throat, "How long ago?" He demanded, "HOW LONG!?"

The demon was barely conscious, head swaying from side to side, as he mumbled "A few days."

"Where did they go?"

The demon's eyes rolled back into his head and he slumped over.

"CHECK THE ENTIRE TRAIN!" He bellowed.

Twenty demons entered the train, searching every cabin and car, they emerged with 4 whisperers holding them by the arms.

"Is he with you?" asked Azazel, motioning to the passed-out demon.

"Yes," one of the demons answered, "but we haven't seen him for days."

"Did you see who hit him? Who was he working on?"

"No, we stay mainly in the bar, but we're missing another."

"HOW LONG?"

"A few days, just like him. We were headed for New Orleans and this one and the other went missing. The other one was messing with an older woman trying to get her to jump."

"EVERYONE ON THE TRAIN!" Azazel ordered them. "Hounds, keep your noses out the windows!"

The train left the station with over a hundred gatherers on board. All trying to ignore the stench of humans all around them, some vomiting violently, others gagging and scrambling for the air outside the train. They rode with their heads out the windows, noses up, sniffing for any scent of the three.

Azazel and the other Nephilim went to the bar to scout for humans they could possess and get warm. They found a group of car salesmen headed for a convention in New Orleans, drinking and laughing and heckling any poor female who happened into the lounge car. The demons settled in and warmed up, "Time for some fun!" Azazel said.

Azazel picked the largest man he could find in the car. He was already drunk and slobbering over the female bartender. The man's eyes turned black as Azazel entered him. The atmosphere in the lounge car changed, it suddenly got cold and the fun and laughing turned to an eerie silence.

The bartender noticed the change in the man's eyes, and his previous fun-loving attitude turned suddenly dark and violent. She had seen this before and knew trouble was coming.

Azazel started, "I'll bet you're a real snob, aren't you? Too good for everyone," he slurred.

"Time for coffee?" She said cautiously.

"Coffee? No, it's time for chaos!" He looked at her and winked.

He turned to everyone in the lounge and yelled

"WHO THINKS THIS SNOB IS TOO GOOD FOR ME?"

The other patrons in the car went silent staring at the large man. He spotted a man drinking coffee near the door.

"What's wrong with you? Have a drink like a real man!" He egged him on, "Or is this wench your wife?" He laughed standing up and started staggering towards the man.

Three other men stood up and blocked his approach.

"Why don't you go sleep it off, we don't want any trouble," one said.

Without warning Azazel hit the man in the face with the glass he was holding. The glass broke and slashed into the man's cheek, his blood began gushing down his face, onto his shirt. The other two men jumped on Azazel's back, at the same time the other demons suddenly started hitting people without warning, smashing glasses and turning over tables. One grabbed the bartender and threw her across the room, slamming her head against the mirror hanging on the wall. The glass shattered, slicing her arm and she fell to the floor. The demon jumped on top of her and started tearing at her clothes, she was terrified as he tore at her blouse. She looked at his eyes hoping to find some kind of compassion, but they were just solid black. Her arm was bleeding as she tried to defend herself. A man jumped on the demon and knocked him to the ground, he climbed on top of the demon and began punching him in the face repeatedly. She climbed to her feet and ran for the emergency box behind the bar. The whole bar was fighting, everyone was fighting everyone, glasses where flying, chairs were being thrown across the room, people were screaming and running for the door.

Suddenly Azazel heard a loud howl, then another, then a hundred hounds were howling at the same time. They had caught the scent! Just then, the bartender reached the emergency stop button and slammed it as hard as she could. The signal reached the engine room and the conductor slammed on the brakes, and everyone in the lounge was thrown forward and off their feet. The wheels began to screech and spark as the train slowed to a crawl. The bartender was on the phone with the conductor now, yelling at him to call the police and send help to the lounge car. As the train slowed, they were about a mile from the small town where the three had gotten off the train a few days ago.

As help arrived from the other cars, the demons left their host bodies and jumped from the train laughing.

"That was awesome!" Azazel said. "Nothing like a good brawl!"

The police were arriving from the nearby town, along with state patrol officers. While Azazel was questioning the hounds, police were boarding the lounge car and had begun interviewing the bartender and witnesses. They called for ambulances and Azazel watched as they hand cuffed the large man, who looked confused and was saying, "I don't remember anything! I didn't do it! Please! I'll lose my job! Miss..." he said, turning to the bartender. "Please! Don't let them arrest me! I'm begging you!"

Azazel smiled, "I should have made him kill the little snot."

He turned and headed for the small town. It occurred to Azazel as he was moving towards town that there was no resistance in the lounge car. He stopped and turned back, looking at the train as they were putting the drunks into police cars and ambulances.

"No one tried to stop us," he said out loud. "No angels were there to fight us. There's always a struggle between good and evil. Angels and demons...but no angels? The guy by the door drinking coffee, and the other 'good guys' were proof of the Holy Spirit's presence, but he's always here..."

Azazel wondered, *if no angels are here, can I kill anyone I want?*

As they reached the small town, the scent took them to the abandoned gas station. Inside, written on one of the walls in large black letters were the words, HELL HOUNDERS. Azazel knowing of this small but powerful group, sighed.

"Miguel," he said out loud.

Sodom and Gomorrah, a wonderful place, Azazel thought. His memory sparked by Miguel's name. *We had everything we wanted there, men... women... animals. Those cities were ours, we had our way with anyone we wanted!* He was smiling at the memories. He remembered the day the two showed up at the gate, Lot, that miserable excuse of a servant and his wife, she deserved to be a pillar of salt! God should have made pillars out of all of them! He destroyed the whole city and the entire valley! That was the beginning of the end, he should have seen it coming, a year later he was cold. So cold for so long now.

He didn't know Miguel and Pedro personally, but he had seen their handy work and liked their style. *But if the three they were chasing were with Miguel and Pedro,* he thought, *this was a game changer, it's not just a stranded angel and the Holy Spirit anymore. This means the big guns are out, it also means Lucifer is underestimating the whole event, just like he underestimated the rebellion and God's response and Golgotha.* No, he was convinced, now more than ever, something's not right here. He needed to get to this stranded angel and find out who he was. He would get this angel for Lucifer, and let him fall into this trap, but with this gap in time, the two humans might be the better hostages.

CHAPTER 14
5 Feet 8 Inches of Hellfire

Amy, the small blonde haired, blue eyed, twenty-seven-year-old who was spoiled beyond redemption rolled through people's lives like a cannon ball. She was a little ball of hellfire.

No one was immune to her fits of 'I want it now' attitude. Did I mention she once made a nun swear? Well it's true, she did! The poor nun had to be transferred to a small village in Madagascar for some well-deserved 'quiet time'.

Amy had an unlimited supply of money and an arsenal of insults at the ready and called on them quite frequently. Once she overcame the initial shock to her system of being somewhat dead, and conquering the fear that the demons had brought, she would be a force to be reckoned with. All by herself. Hell hath no fury like Amy scorned!

The group traveled the side roads, making their way to the airport in Alexandria. They had stopped in a small town called Irma, just outside of Natchitoches, Louisiana. At a small gas station, the six travelers all got out to stretch their legs and get some fresh air. The storm was still moving through the area, it was cold and raining, and a winter chill was in the air. Amy wandered inside the store out of boredom, and the need to be away from the smell of the old van. Chewy followed her in, to stock his satchel.

It was so warm inside the store, and she had been cold all day. The heater in the old van was terrible and it smelled like dust. She wandered the aisles, avoiding patrons, and wondered if she should knock things off shelves just to mess with people's minds a little. Chewy was a few aisles over gathering his necessities, it made him happy to think of feeding all his friends. Amy came across a young girl, maybe fifteen years old. She looked dirty and tired, her hair was a mess, and her makeup was smeared as if she had been crying. The girl was standing at the end of an aisle, she could also see an older man in his late 30's standing close by. He was saying something to the girl, so Amy moved closer to listen,

"I have a phone charger in my car outside," he was saying. "You're welcome to use it, you can stay warm for a little while...I mean, while it's charging."

As Amy glanced over the man's shoulder she could barely make out someone else standing close behind the man. Then she saw him, a whisperer was leaning in close to the man's ear, she could hear him saying "Take this little pig out to the car, we'll take her to our place in the woods where we took the other pigs. Tell her we can give her a ride too, anywhere she needs."

"I can give you a ride if you need, anywhere you want. It's better than freezing to death!" The man said, just as suggested.

The girl was a runaway, Lizzy Hamilton, she was fifteen years old a small brunette from Dallas. She had hitchhiked with her friend Kimberly. They had decided to go to a boy's house that Lizzy had met online, in Baton Rouge. But her girlfriend had left her here all alone, to go with a boy she had met at the café last night. She was all alone and had no idea what to do. Her phone was dead, and she had no money, they had spent their last six dollars on food last night. She had gone into the gas station to get warm. The man she was talking to was a guy from another small town nearby, Mark Joiner. He was a predator; his mode of operation was to cruise small towns in the area and pick up young girls on the run.

They were so easy for him, as he wasn't bad looking. He wore dreadlocks, and was unshaven most of the time, and still somewhat young enough for these younger girls to still want to talk to him. He knew hunger and fear was his best approach, or cigarettes, or maybe pot, whatever the bait needed to be, or worked the best.

Five girls so far had taken the bait, all were dead. He had a demon that stayed close to him, and this whisperer was getting very good at talking Mark into almost anything. The more he killed, the easier it got, his human was becoming eager to kill. He found that if he compared this human's mother to these harlots, the human would work himself into a compulsive, uncontrollable, insatiable need for death. The desire to control someone's fate was irresistible, and it was easier and easier to achieve with this mindless grunt of a human.

As Amy listened, her heart began to race, the girl was agreeing to go to the man's car! Amy's mind started to race, she had to do something! They were headed to the door now... she couldn't think! ...what should she do? She wanted to scream at the girl, but she wouldn't be heard. She ran up behind the girl and screamed "RUN! RUN NOW!"

The girl was becoming uneasy, she felt a panic begin to rise in her, her head was screaming *RUN! THIS ISN'T RIGHT, RUN!* Amy kept screaming "RUN! RUN NOW!" As Amy screamed, the demon heard her and came bounding out from behind the shelf. He was moving towards her, nose in the air sniffing.

Amy turned back to the girl, her eyes were wide as she was looking at the man, "I don't think...," she began.

The man put his hand in his pocket and said, "Just keep going, it's fine."

She looked into his eyes, they had turned black. The air around him was ice cold, and now she was terrified. He took her arm, then Lizzy's mind began to panic, *RUN, JUST RUN!* She broke free from the man's grip and ran out the door. The man looked around nervously and went out the door slowly, Amy ran past him and followed the girl across the parking lot screaming as she ran, "RUN! KEEP RUNNING!"

Miguel and the others were standing at the gas pump, they heard Amy screaming and they turned and saw a young girl running across the parking lot with Amy close behind her. Then they saw the demon and the man walking quickly towards them, the demon's nose was in the air, sniffing and growling, and it began to run. Miguel lifted his head towards heaven and closed his eyes.

Officer Tony Sniedel sat filling out his paperwork, parked a few blocks away. He had one ear listening to his dispatch radio, as he filled out his forms. He became aware of an uneasy feeling rising in his chest, something wasn't right...he turned down his radio and rolled down his window. He didn't know what it was, but he was suddenly feeling nervous and anxious, so he leaned his head out the window slightly and listened. The uneasiness was growing in his chest...he listened some more...he didn't know why, but he started his car and turned onto the road. He began to drive, window down, slowly at first. The feeling in his stomach was getting unbearable. He turned onto the main street and headed toward the gas station at the end of town, his sense of urgency growing.

As Amy ran toward the girl the demon closed the gap between them, she could hear his feet pounding on the wet concrete. The anger inside of Amy was growing with every step, she imagined what they were going to do to this girl, the anger boiled up in her and her face turned red.

She turned just as the demon reached her, she hit the demon with her fist squarely on the nose as hard as she could. She felt the bone in his nose break under her fist. The demon stopped in his tracks, he took a step back and shook his head, green slime started to gush from his nose.

The man approached the girl. As Amy ran up to him she didn't know what she was going to do but she had to try! She got close, so she could see his eyes, they weren't blue any more they were black! Completely black! She froze...a Nephilim! *Oh God, they found us*!

Just then Officer Sniedel pulled into the parking lot. He saw a man approaching a young girl, and she looked frightened. He pulled his car in between the girl and the man. As he got out of his car his heart was

~ 113 ~

pumping, still anxious, he drew his weapon and ordered the man to stop.

"Hands out of your pocket! He shouted. The man raised one hand. "What? What did I do?"

"Both hands up where I can see them. NOW!" The officer ordered.

The demon screamed "SHOOT HIM! SHOOT HIM! HE'S GONNA KILL YOU!"

The man pulled the weapon out and fired. It happened so fast officer Sniedel didn't have time to react. The bullet hit him directly in the center of the chest, it felt like he had been hit with a bat, and it knocked him backward off his feet, he stumbled and hit the ground. Shock! Terror! His family raced across his mind. *My vest,* he thought, *did my vest stop it?* He didn't realize he was still pointing his gun at the man, his eyes wouldn't or couldn't focus. He could see the figure approaching him gun raised to fire again.

Amy saw Pedro slam the demon to the ground, hitting him fast and hard, time and time again. Then, for a very brief second, less than a second, she saw an angel. Not Leahcim, not Miguel, but an angel, dressed all in white. A very large man was standing between Officer Sniedel and the man with the gun, the angel was holding a sword that was on fire!

The man was firing his gun as fast as he could pull the trigger, his bullets hit the sword and sparked, and then the angel was gone. Tony fired his gun, two, three, four rounds hit the man. He stopped and dropped down to his knees, he sat there with his head down breathing heavily. He raised his head and looked at the officer, and then beyond him at the girl. He raised his gun again, this time pointed at the girl.

The demon started screaming under Pedro, "SHOOT THAT PIG! ONE MORE... GET ONE MORE!"

Tony Sniedel's next bullet hit the man between the eyes, his head snapped back as the bullet tore through his skull, and he fell back onto the wet concrete.

Amy watched the Nephilim leave the man's body, it was just a dark presence that swooped upward into the night air and then was gone.

Tony fell backward onto the pavement, he turned his head as he lay there, his heart still racing out of control. He saw Pedro on top of what looked like a man, but he was naked and pale with grotesque features. Pedro was still beating the demon, it turned its head and looked at Tony, Tony would swear it was smiling at him. Pedro finally let the demon up and it ran off into the night, Tony watched as it disappeared into the darkness. He reached for his shoulder radio and said in a fading voice, "Shots fired...officer down."

The six travelers watched as the parking lot filled with police cars and ambulances, in what seemed like seconds. Amy stayed next to the young girl and listened as she called her father, "Daddy, I want to come home. Will you come get me?" Amy could hear the joy in her father's voice, "As fast as I can honey, as fast as I can!"

Amy had found something inside herself that she didn't know was there. She watched as they loaded Tony into the ambulance, and as the young girl was put into a police car. She watched as they loaded the dead man's body into a black bag and zipped it closed. She had suddenly become human, she realized she could no longer watch the world from the protection of her detached bubble of existence. These were real people, they lived real lives, painful heartbreaking lives!

"God, this hurts," she said out loud. "God, why does this hurt so much?" She envisioned in her mind someone sticking a pin into her bubble and she saw it explode. And she felt, for the first time ever, she felt that her life had been a waste. Amy made a decision at that very moment that she would never be that same cold, callus little rich girl again. In her heart, and quietly in her mind she said a prayer. She asked God to forgive her for all the years she had wasted, for all the pain she had caused others. She felt a deep sense of shame for the way she had lived, and she never wanted to cause anyone any pain ever again. She wanted...God.

As she raised her head from that little quiet prayer that no one, but God heard, she sensed an odd change sweep over her. A strange peace, she felt a new presence inside her. She looked at Miguel in wonder... she wanted that thing he had, that thing that surrounded him. Amy suddenly felt a new connection with him, which was unexplainable. She knew somehow, he had a power within him, that he was somehow more than he had said he was.

CHAPTER 15
And the Meek Shall Inherit the Earth

Johnathan was twenty-nine years old. He was somewhat shy, he didn't care much for confrontation, unless it was with Amy. This whole dead thing had brought out some deep resentment toward her and her father. As far as humans go he was rather meek, not in a weak way, but in an 'I just want to be left alone' way.

Life for Johnathan had become mundane, his sense of adventure had been lost in the ocean when he was twelve. His parents died when he was eighteen, both killed in a car accident, that event had torn his world apart. He had finished high school and started college but dropped out when he couldn't manage to feed himself and go to school anymore. He worked odd jobs for a few years, and finally landed the job with Amy's father.

When he died a few days ago, he realized how angry he actually was, that he had let her father basically have his life. He would realize, before this was over, that his anger which was currently being taken out on Amy, was in fact not against her, or her father, but against God himself. Johnathan did believe that there was a God, but he didn't like him. He would soon come to terms with this, and in no uncertain terms let God know how he felt. The great thing about God is, He's a really good listener.

Johnathan was asleep in the back of the van when they stopped at the gas station. He heard everyone pile out and decided to keep sleeping. Leahcim stayed in the van with Johnathan and was reading his manual, yet again, hoping he'd missed something.

"RUN, KEEP RUNNING!" They both heard the screams from Amy. Johnathan opened his eyes and looked at Leahcim.

"What's going on?" He asked.

"I'm not sure," Leahcim replied.

They both slid out of the side door, opposite the commotion. Leahcim didn't feel the blow to his head, everything just went dark.

Johnathan felt a cold slimy hand go across his mouth and chest. *Dark ones!* He thought.

The four dark ones had come up to gather Mark's soul, but two of them smelled out Johnathan. These two were aware of the bounty on the three, and they had slipped away from the other two gatherers. They'd decided to grab Leahcim and hide him until they could get back to Lucifer. They snuck up behind him them, and knocked Leahcim out, and grabbed Johnathan. They dragged Johnathan across the field as the others were distracted by current events unfolding in the parking lot.

About a mile away from the gas station was a large horse ranch. The demons pulled Johnathan, fighting and struggling, across the field and into a large horse stable. There they threw him into one of the horse stalls and locked the door. The stall was wood half way up and bars covered the upper half of the door. It was the perfect holding place while the two demons figured out their plan.

These two demons weren't like the other gatherers Johnathan had seen. They were both wearing dingy, dirty, torn robes... what used to be white robes.

While they were mean and ill-tempered like the others, they seemed to have some semblance of intelligence. They also seemed to appear a little more like humans than demons. They walked more upright and weren't as deformed as the others that Johnathan had seen.

Johnathan moved to the back of the stall, heart pounding, and listened as they plotted.

Zuek and Imlack were smarter than most, as far as demons go. They were assigned as gatherers and they felt slighted by Lucifer. They still had good eyes and ears and relatively lucid thought patterns. For centuries now the two had flown under Lucifer's radar, doing as little gathering as possible, and plotting as often as they could, waiting for their opportunity. The two wanted to be higher up in the food chain, out of the gatherers stench pen and into the world of plotters. They wanted to be managing the activities of the whisperers and other demonic activities. This was their chance to bargain their way up.

Zuek had an even greater plan he had been scheming now for some time, Imlack was smart, but in the end, he was loyal to Lucifer.

"We've waited long enough!" Imlack said.

"Don't be stupid Imlack, this is the moment we've been hoping for," replied Zuek.

"He'll give us what we want, and as soon as he sees this smelly rat we'll get our promotion. They put out a reward!" Imlack argued.

"The other idiots would be at Lucifer's door already claiming their reward, we need to lay low and let Lucifer get more desperate for them." Zuek replied.

"Two hundred and forty-nine years Zuek. We've been waiting two hundred and forty-nine years for this!"

"And ten more days, or two more years won't matter if we get a better reward." Zuek said.

Imlack was tapping his long fingernails on the door of Johnathan's stall, looking at him with contempt. "It's rumored we can kill him you know," Imlack said.

"Good idea, let's kill him and spend eternity burning in the pit now! Why wait?" Zuek said sarcastically. "Look, if we wait this out I know Lucifer will offer more. I heard he called in the Nephilim. If that's true, then there's something different about this guy, he's worth a lot more than just a promotion."

"How long?" Imlack asked.

"As long as it takes. Look you head back out there and watch. Go back to the gas station and hide out, just watch and listen. Stay on top of them. I'll stay here with this." He pointed at Johnathan snidely. "Come back if you hear anything new from Lucifer."

Imlack swore under his breath and left the stable.

Zuek walked over to the stall and looked in at Johnathan, "You're going to change my whole existence." He moved away from the stall and took a position by the door. Leaning up against the wall he slid down onto the floor, with knees up and head perched, he looked out into the field.

Johnathan had watched the two exchange words, and he worried about what Imlack had said about killing him. He hadn't realized until now that these things were actual *beings*, not human, but they had some kind of reasoning. They were self-aware beings with flesh of sorts and some brains. He wondered what their existence had been like before, when they were angels, and how different it must be for them now after the fall. He moved closer to the door of the stall.

"Hey," he said, looking at Zuek, in a half-terrified voice.

Zuek turned his head toward Johnathan and growled in a low tone.

"Would you talk to me?" He asked, his voice still slightly trembling. There was a long silence....

"What could we possibly talk about human?" Zuek said.

"What's your name, do you have a name?"

Another long silence

"Zuek," he grumbled.

"I'm Johnathan."

"I know your name, human."

Johnathan swallowed hard and looked at the floor. "Do you miss it?" Johnathan asked.

"Miss what?"

"Heaven...God?"

There was a very long silence, Zuek was looking out the doorway, arms resting on his knees. In a barely audible voice he answered without looking at Johnathan, "Yes."

Zuek didn't turn to look at Johnathan he just kept looking out at the field, and he raised his head and smelled the air. The smell of the freshly plowed earth, the rich soil, reminded him of heaven. He hated this life... or whatever this was. He longed for the air of heaven and to fly again, to spread his wings as wide as he could, and soar. He looked at the ground and his heart ached. Anger began to fill him, the thought of being here, separated from God forever.

"Why did you do it? I mean why did you turn against Him?" Johnathan asked meekly.

He jumped to his feet and ran at the stall, slamming his fist against the door.

"YOU! YOU'RE THE REASON I'M HERE! HUMANS!"

Johnathan stumbled back from the door, eyes wide, heart pounding again.

"Do you realize, human, that there was nothing bad in heaven? Nothing evil until He created you!! Never a murder, a beating, nothing! You brought these things! NOT US!" He was pacing back and forth now. He was calming himself, still talking. "We were his first creation not you. We were who He cherished, and we worshiped Him, we ministered to Him day and night! All that he asked or required, we did!" His voice got louder as he was getting angry. "Then we found out that there were to be more created ones, different ones, better ones...you. You were created a little lower than us, but you humans, the ones that would believe and follow the law would be brought to heaven to rule with Him. Even over us! He wanted a creation that would *choose* to be with him."

Johnathan hadn't moved from the corner of the stall, he stood silent, listening. He didn't dare look at Zuek.

Zuek, still pacing continued, "This was Lucifer's plan, the rebellion idea, he said God's plan would never work. That he could prove to God that we were the better creation, that you would never make it out of Eden! So we all agreed, and Lucifer went without God's knowing into the garden, and the next thing I know, we're falling, smashed against the earth, CAST OUT!"

"So he tricked you into following?" Johnathan almost whispering.

"No, well yes, SORT OF! He didn't tell us he was planning on removing God from the throne. He was just supposed to *prove* to God that His plan was flawed! But WHAT HE REALLY WANTED was to dominate the world and have everyone, and everything, worship HIM!"

"What happened when you got here?"

"Everything changed. We now had dominion over the earth... you know, 'princes and principalities the rulers of this earth'... and Lucifer convinced us that we could still win." He sighed heavily, he was back at the doorway, and he slid back down the frame onto the floor.

He picked up a piece of horse manure and started eating it like an apple. Johnathan looked away and gagged.

Zuek continued "I knew though, on that day, I knew it!... I knew we were lost forever."

"What day?"

"Golgotha," his head slumped between his knees as he answered.

"Golgotha, what's Golgotha?"

"The place of the scull." Johnathan could hardly hear him, his voice was soft and somber.

"Lucifer said this was it, that he had defeated God, that God's plan was flawed and that he had caused God's creations to deny Him. And that the creation would kill the creator! He had trapped the Son of Man. And he whispered in the ear of the Pharisees, the Sanhedrin and the Sadducees that he had gotten into the inner circle of the Son. He said he had him betrayed by one of his own, and that we were going to win, and God's plan had failed, that we had finally beaten him."

"You mean the crucifixion?"

"Yes, this was it, but I knew. I saw it as we turned the corner from the theater where we beat him. I saw them as we tied the beam across his arms. I looked up at the scull, and I saw them gathering, all in their white robes slowly gathering in silence. The dust from the chariots and riders was filling the sky, they never said a word, they just kept coming, millions of them. As we walked up the hill, I knew something was wrong." Zuek never looked up, the whole time he was talking, he never looked into Johnathan's eyes. He just looked forward.

"What, what did you see?"

"A million angels, ten million... everywhere... the entire Army of God was there. Horses and riders lined every hilltop, alongside the chariots of God, thousands and thousands of them. Archers all with full quivers of arrows were on every building looking down, watching. Swordsmen lined the streets two and three deep, their swords remained in their sheaths. Spearmen in ranks were in every field, shields held tightly against their chests. They were in every window and on top of every home, and in the market. The walls of the city where white with them... so many angels... and not a single sword was drawn, not a spear was cast. And all were silent. The riders could hardly contain their horses... that's when I knew, when they didn't fight, they just let it happen." He dropped his head again between his legs...there was a long pause.

"Everybody was so happy, dancing, whispering in the ears of the romans, Lucifer was trying to get to Mary, but the Guardians were too strong they held him back, he just kept running in front of the Son taunting him." Zuek raised his head and closed his eyes, "Oh Lucifer you fool!" He said, grinding his teeth. "Lucifer kept running up to the angels and taunting them too... "FIGHT! THIS IS YOUR KING!

FIGHT!" He was yelling at them, but they didn't budge. They never flinched. I saw his smile fade at one point, I think it crossed his mind that he had made a mistake. He stopped and looked at the hilltops and buildings, to the sea of white, we were outnumbered three to one, they could have killed every one of us. They had swords and spears, horses and chariots with flaming wheels... we had sticks and clubs." Zuek shook his head.

"We watched as they crucified him. A million demons cheered and danced and heckled his disciples." Zuek went silent as he remembered.

He thought carefully before he spoke again, it was a long time before he began again.

"I was at the foot of the cross, the other demons had gathered in so close we were almost on top of each other. They pushed me down to the ground... and I saw the first drop of blood as it hit the ground" ...another pregnant pause...

"I stared at it as it disappeared into the ground. I swear I heard the earth groan. And then I felt the rumble, and then the whole earth shook so violently, and the lightning started...," he paused. "I looked at Lucifer and I knew that I knew then. He realized what had really just happened.

He had a look on his face, he was pale, and his mouth kind of dropped open... he stumbled backward and looked up at the Son, hanging there in the rain... and he just kind of turned around and wandered off into the storm." Zuek shook his head sadly and looked back outside.

Johnathan was engrossed in the story, he was holding onto the bars of the stall, waiting for more. Finally, he said, "I don't understand, what did just happen? Are you saying you killed the Son of God?"

Zurek's head snapped around to look at Johnathan. "HE GAVE HIMSELF! WE WERE DECIEVED! NO GREATER LOVE AND ALL THAT CRAP! HE LAID DOWN HIS LIFE FOR *YOU STUPID HUMANS*! I COULD

CARE LESS ABOUT WHO HE WAS, HE WAS MEANINGLESS TO ME!" Zuek was shaking, he was so irate.

"Do you know how ironic that question is?" Zuek said. "This event was supposed to keep you from ever reaching God. Instead you can go freely to him now... no law, no deed is too bad. DON'T YOU GET IT? NOTHING YOU DO NOW CAN KEEP YOU OUT! NOTHING!! ALL BECAUSE OF A SINGLE DROP OF BLOOD!"

He was at the stall door again, shaking the bars in anger.

"DON'T YOU GET IT? IT WAS THE PLAN ALL ALONG!" Zuek yelled. "IT WAS A SET-UP ALL ALONG! FROM THE BEGINNING! THE LAW, THE BLOOD SACRIFICES, MOSES, DAVID, GIDEON, ALL THE PROPHETS! WE WERE SET UP FROM DAY ONE OF CREATION!" He was up and pacing back and forth now.

"He knew, all along what would happen. He knew Lucifer would be tempted by the glory. He knew we would follow him. He knew the cross was our ultimate end. ALL OF THIS!!!" He gestured toward his own body, "ALL OF THIS... TORMENT...IS BECAUSE OF YOU!!"

He ran at the stall and slammed his fist against the door "I SWEAR TO YOU HUMAN...I WILL TAKE AS MANY OF YOU AS I CAN!" He shook the bars on the door violently and turned and stomped out of the barn.

Johnathan was left alone and trembling. He realized after the encounter with Zuek that his knees were actually shaking, and he felt sick to his stomach. He moved back across the stall and slid down the wall. He sat there eyes wide, his mind spinning and racing. This was the first time he had been alone since all this started, it was quiet, and he could hear his heart still pounding from the encounter. He wanted to cry. Tears began to well up in his eyes, all this emotion started flooding in "ARRGHHH!" He screamed and pounded his fist into the floor.

"WHAT?! WHAT DO YOU WANT FROM ME?! I DON'T EVEN KNOW WHO... TELL ME WHAT YOU WANT!? YOU KILLED MY PARENTS WASN'T THAT ENOUGH? HUH? WASN'T IT?! YOU WANT MORE! IS

THAT IT?" Johnathan was shaking with emotion as he yelled at the top of his lungs, demanding answers. "LET'S SEE WHAT ELSE CAN WE DO TO JOHNATHAN! OH, I KNOW LET'S KILL HIM TOO, ONLY NOT REALLY!! TELL ME WHAT YOU WANT!!"

His face was red, bordering on purple, and the veins were bulging in his neck. Johnathan had never yelled at anyone in his life. This needed to come out, and it needed to come out now at this moment.

"SO YOU'RE GOD HUH? THE BIG BAD SQUASH WHOEVER I WANT GOD!"

He was getting tired and his voice was softening, he began to weep as he slid back down the wall, in defeat.

"I don't understand this. This is so hard! Why are you doing this to me? I KNOW I'VE SCREWED UP EVERTHING IN MY LIFE! Just tell me what you want...please, God. Just tell me."

At this moment, in Johnathan's heart, (and in every man or woman's heart) one of two things will happen. Your heart hardens, and you never come to God. Or... God in His mercy and grace softens your heart and brings you to a place you've never been before...on your knees.

CHAPTER 16
Secrets

Lucifer felt the spirit of Mark leave his body and sent four gatherers to collect one of his prize students. He feels every spirit that enters and departs from this world. The new ones are off limits, he isn't allowed to 'play' with their minds until the year of reckoning, around twelve or thirteen years old, after that they're fair game. The old spirits are collectable at the time of death. It's a lot like dragging bodies off the battle field.

The gatherers waited for Mark's spirit to rise from his body. The body bag began to move, the gatherers looked at each other and smiled.

"This is my favorite part," one of them said as he looked on, rubbing his hands together. Mark sat up violently, he looked all around and then spotted the two gatherers. He stood up and looked at the body bag. The gatherers were on him fast, each one taking him by an arm. He started shaking his head and explaining.

"I wasn't going to do anything," he said in a panicked voice, looking back and forth from demon to demon, looking for some compassion from either one.

"Yes, you were," one of the demons replied.

"No, I was just going to help her."

The coroner was loading his body bag on to a stretcher. The demons began pulling him away from the scene.

"NO! WAIT! I DIDN'T DO ANYTHING!" He was begging.

"PLEASE! DON'T DO THIS, I CAN FIX THIS! GIVE ME ANOTHER CHANCE!"

"Not unless you can raise the others from the grave." The demon laughed.

"Lucifer is waiting, he's very proud of what you've done." The other demon said in a cynical tone.

In a normal situation, if heaven were open now, angels would have been present at this gathering of Marks soul. They would have escorted Mark and the gatherers to the shallow graves that Mark had placed his victims in. In silence, they would have moved from grave to grave as Mark relived each death. This exercise is a powerful reminder of one's life and leaves little doubt in their minds as to their fate, it goes without saying.

Miguel was still standing arms spread wide, head back with his eyes closed, a slight smile grew across his face.

"There jou are my friend, it's ok we're coming," he said under his breath.

Amy and Pedro had moved back to the van and stood next to Miguel. They watched the gatherers take Mark away, cross the road and head for Lucifer's camp.

Chewy found Leahcim lying beside the van, he ran around the other side and stomped his foot on the ground and motioned for Miguel and the others. As Leahcim began to regain consciousness he mumbled, "Oh the staircase, I've missed the staircase!"

Miguel kneeling next to him said, "Leahcim... Leahcim," softly tapping him on the cheek.

"What happened?" Leahcim asked.

"A lot my friend, jou missed some good action."

Amy looking in the van said, "Where's Johnathan? Leahcim, where's Johnathan?"

"I don't know, we got out of the van when we heard you yelling and that's the last I remember."

Miguel looked at Leahcim and said, "Take a stone my friend and cast it toward those two running across the field. I have found our Jewish friend, but he has a problem. We need to confuse these demons, or they'll bring back trouble. Cover all the demons nearby."

He said it as if Leahcim understood the instructions, in a matter of fact kind of way.

These spirits were used usually by God. He very often used these tools to confuse, or even deceive the enemy. God had equipped every angel with these stones as an emergency measure to throw off demons, and sometimes even Lucifer.

As Leahcim drew the stone and threw it toward the demons, a spirit of confusion left the stone and spread out over the field and surrounding area. It was an amber colored wave as it traveled, and it would give off a brief red and white glow as it struck its intended target. They watched as it spread out across the field... the whisperer was hit first, and then the wave continued. As it reached the two demons with Mark, they saw the red spurt, then it caught Imlack in the tree line, another red glow. Then higher up off the ground it caught a fourth - the Nephilim that had overtaken Mark. Then they watched as it traveled, it came to the buildings in the distance and passed through them, they saw it glow again as it hit Zuek. Then the night was lit up as it hit dozens around the buildings, and they watched as it traveled out of sight.

Miguel turned to the group and said, "He's over there." He pointed to the farm.

They all piled into the van and headed in that direction. As they pulled in they were met by a kind old gentleman named Zeek. Zeek and his wife Grace had owned the horse farm since they were newlyweds, fifty-six years ago. Miguel got out and greeted Zeek and asked if they rented stalls for horse boarding? As Zeek began to answer Miguel's question with a long and very detailed explanation of how the farm came to be, the rest of the group got out of the van and spread out in search of Johnathan.

Lucifer was laying on his couch in his office, eyes closed, concentrating on the image he had of Amy and Johnathan. If he thought hard enough he could drift off into a place where he could find dreams connected to an individual having the dream. If the person was currently dreaming he could infiltrate the dream, like he had done with Amy. As he was laying there he heard a cry go out to God. It was Johnathan! Lucifer's eyes opened wide, "Got ya!" He said out loud. He closed his eyes again and concentrated. He listened as Johnathan yelled at God, the same thing they always say...poor me, look what you've done to me, always me me me! That's what he loved about these humans, their self-absorption. Although it was an easy way in for him, he had to be careful, when they're crying out to God it's usually their first step to coming to Him. But they're very vulnerable right then, so they're easily turned. He had to get to him!

Johnathan was laying on his side in the horse stall. After his argument with God and the exchange with Zuek, he was emotionally exhausted, and he had drifted off to sleep.

"He's not listening," it was a soft voice Johnathan heard, "he's never been listening to you."

Johnathan was sitting in a small boat barely big enough to hold him, and it was drifting, rocking back and forth. He could smell the water and felt it hit his fingers as he held tightly to both sides of the boat. He was scared... he couldn't see land, and he didn't like water.

"You know that feeling you have in the pit of your stomach, that one you've always had?" The voice said. Johnathan knew the feeling he was referring to, it made him feel sick and ashamed. He hated it. It told him he was worthless, inferior to everyone else and of little value to anyone.

"That's how he sees you. That's what he really thinks of you. He put that feeling in you," there was a long pause. "Oh sure, he *says* he loves everyone, and he does I suppose...everyone but you! ... Do you think he meant it when he said he would never leave you?" Lucifer was referring to a promise God made to his children.

"You have to be a child of God I suppose for that one," Lucifer continued. "He has no use for you."

In the corner of his eye Johnathan saw a figure, very small, very far off in the distance. A man dressed in a brown robe, with dull blue and red stripes, he was just standing on the water looking toward Johnathan. Johnathan could feel his presence, but the man didn't say anything he was just there.

"This boat won't save you, it's not big enough. I can save you though," Johnathan felt a cold wet hand touch his, he pulled it back quickly and held it tight against his chest. The boat began to rock violently.

Then far away Johnathan heard a small voice yelling across the water. "God is my defender, I will not be moved." ...and again..." God is my defender, I will not be moved!" The voice was so far away, he looked out into the water, it was Leahcim. He was pointing across the water to the other man, who was standing on the water.

"Don't look at him, LOOK AT ME!! I'll save you, take my hand!"

"God is my defender...," the voice was louder and closer, "...I will not be moved." Johnathan looked to the man in the robe, still standing far away, just looking at Johnathan. His presence was peaceful, "God is my..." Johnathan started, his voice was unsure and unsteady.

"DON'T EVEN TRY JOHNATHAN!" Lucifer yelled. "HE'S NOT YOUR DEFENDER, I AM! IT WONT WORK FOR YOU!"

Johnathan closed his eyes and screamed, "GOD IS MY DEFENDER... I WILL NOT BE MOVED!" His fingers clenching the sides of the boat.

"Five minutes ago you were calling him out, and now he's your savior? Gimme a break!" Lucifer turned towards the man on the water and growled

Johnathan woke with a start and sat halfway up. His first thought was of the man in the robe on the water, and then he felt calm, he wasn't scared.

"Who are you?" A voice said.

Johnathan looked up, it was Zuek. He was kneeling, picking up horse manure and eating it again as fast as he could. Johnathan watched and gagged as the demon ate.

"I've been watching you sleeping. Do I know you?" Zuek said as he slid across the floor on his knees and put his face next to Johnathan's. "Do I?"

Johnathan could smell the manure on his breath and recoiled and covered his nose.

"Want some?" He held out his hand to Johnathan. "It's hard to find good ones here." Zuek moved back to the stall door and stood up, looking around he yelled "OH, WHERE IS ALL THE GOOD PRODUCE? I've been thinking," he started, and just then Amy swung a shovel as hard as she could, striking Zuek in the back of the head. He flew to the side and smashed his face into the side of the stall door.

"AMY!" Johnathan shouted.

Lucifer's eyes flew open. "ZUEK!" He sat up quickly. "You're keeping secretes my little goblin friend! And that angel... I hate that guy!"

"Oh man am I glad to see you!" Johnathan said.

"Wow this guy smells like you." Amy pointed to Zuek. "You two have the same diet I see."

Johnathan jumped up, and to Amy's shock, grabbed her and hugged her.

"Ok don't get all Jesus on me," she said.

"I think I saw him."

"Who?" She asked.

Leahcim and the two Mexicans walked into the barn. "Johnathan! You're ok!" Leahcim said. Pedro and chewy smiled and high fived each other.

"You won't believe what this guy told me," Johnathan said.

"Lies, I would imagine." Leahcim replied.

"I don't think so, he told me about the day of the cross," Johnathan was talking fast and excitedly. "Oh and this dream, you were there I think, pointing at that guy."

Leahcim put his arm around Johnathan's shoulder and turned him towards the door and began walking him to the van as Johnathan rambled on.

They found Miguel resting his chin on his arm leaning onto the van, still listening to Zeek give his account of how the Farm came to be. He straightened and smiled at the group as they approached, "Oh thank the Father," he said in a relieved voice. "Well, thank jou Zeek, we have to go."

"Oh are you leaving? I wanted to tell you about the time the horse kicked me in the head, damndest thing you ever saw."

"Maybe another time my friend, God bless jou."

They were all back together and back on the road. Johnathan, in the back of the van, felt something new inside, something he had never felt before. A strange new feeling and he didn't have that sick feeling in his stomach anymore. Hope maybe, he couldn't quite put his finger on it, it had something to do with his dream and the man on the water. He liked this new feeling, it was like his soul was suddenly.... warm.

CHAPTER 17

The Pit of Hell

Azazel was holding Imlack by the neck about two feet off the ground, his feet swinging back and forth in the air, as he struggled. Lucifer had Zuek's forehead in his hand and was reading his mind. His past thoughts were presenting themselves like a book, Lucifer could see and hear everything Zuek had said and done.

Zuek started to speak, and Lucifer reached down and picked up a large pile of horse manure and shoved it into Zuek's mouth. Then grabbing his jaw with his other hand, he closed Zuek's mouth holding it closed, and lifted him up by the jaw and held him against the stall door.

"Secrets Zuek! Telling and keeping secrets!" Lucifer stepped back from the door, Zuek hung there pinned to the stall door.

"WHERE ARE THEY?!"Lucifer demanded.

Azazel, who had been alerted by the Nephilim, said, "It's a spirit of confusion, they don't remember anything."

"You seem... disenchanted with your lot, as it were, Zuek." Lucifer said.

Zuek's eyes were wide, he tried to speak as the horse manure fell from his mouth.

A black liquid began to ooze up from the ground and started to pool under Zuek's feet. It would flash flames up and go out, then flash again and go out. He could feel the heat of the liquid and flames, and he began to squirm and thrash.

Azazel watched as he continued to hold Imlack in the air.

"If the lake were open!" Lucifer looked into Zuek's eyes as he spoke.

The lake of fire was long ago reserved for Lucifer and his demons. A place of torment for their part in the rebellion and all the evil they have distributed since the fall. Complete separation from God, a destiny they all knew of. It was at this point in their existence the reason they had to follow Lucifer, in futile hope of changing this outcome and winning the battle against God. (Thereby avoiding eternal damnation to the pit of hell.)

"Lets go for a walk shall we, Zuek?" In an instant they were walking in hell. It was hot, the ground under their feet, the stone walls, lit only by the flames of the lake in the distance, were too hot to touch. Azazel liked it, he was warm finally, he could stay here a while, he thought.

Zuek hated it here. It was so humid, miserable, and eerily quiet. He could see people and demons moving around, and there was an impending doom that was thick in the air and everyone felt it. No one spoke, with the exception of an occasional exchange between demons.

Keepers were assigned to watch the entrances lest anyone should be tempted to leave. They were the biggest, ugliest demons that Lucifer could find. The ones with grotesque deformities and too large to be messed with, they stood two to each entrance. The quiet was occasionally broken by a scream, usually a new soul being tormented by an old one. This place was the pit of evil, old souls would eventually reach a point of rage and explode. Finding a new soul and beating them until they could no longer move, breaking bones, knocking out teeth, snapping arms, etcetera. Most new souls would find a rock or cave to hide in, if they were lucky. Food didn't exist and there was virtually no water to be found. Very few demons spent any time here, it was a reminder of what was to come. They dropped off souls and went back to earth or 'top side', as it was called, as fast as possible.

The souls they dropped off would just be released into hell and left to wander. No one talked much... souls that is. They understood when they arrived what had happened, and conversations by nature, convey hope of some kind. The kids, the job, the new house, a new car, the weather, the next trip...those things in this place, are all gone. Hope is all gone.

The two gatherers were approaching Lucifer with Mark in tow. The gatherers smiled as they placed Mark in front of Lucifer.

"Don't look at me that way," Lucifer said.

They always had the same look on their face, pitiful droopy eyes, head held low. It was a hopeless blank stare of... well, indescribable despair. And there was no cure.

Mark started, "Je...," and stopped.

"What was that?" Lucifer said.

"Jesus?" Mark said in almost a whisper.

"THERE IT IS!" Lucifer shouted.

"Too late for that one buddy! You had your whole life to claim that prize pal, you're here by your own choice! Unfortunately, God did not send you here, neither did I for that matter! This was entirely your choice! If God sent all of you here, that should be here, He would be sitting there twiddling his thumbs." He halfway mumbled.

He was telling the truth for the first time in a long time. God has in fact never sent anyone to hell. The only way to hell is by one's very own choice. A choice He gave you, he will not force anyone to believe.

Lucifer took Mark by the arm and started walking. Mark looked around at his new surroundings, it was so hot and humid, and he noticed he didn't sweat, he wished he could sweat! It was just hot!

As they walked, Mark could see people walking... barefoot, naked, dirty. They all walked alone, not in groups or even in pairs, always alone. They would look at him and quickly look back at the ground and hurry away. He saw them in caves and on rock ledges, some with obvious injuries that would not heal, and the weeping, he could hear weeping and cries of anguish, they always seemed to be off in the distance, but they never stopped. He couldn't see them, but he heard them, they seemed to be just around each bend. He noticed that there were no children here, he saw young men and women, middle aged, and old ones, but no children.

"I know what you're thinking," Lucifer said. "No kids, too bad huh? A guy like you...a place like this...think of the fun you could have." Lucifer smirked.

"Why?"

"No, they're the only truly innocent ones. God keeps them for Himself, we don't get those."

"Where do I go... I mean where should I stay?" Mark asked, he was scared, still shaking.

"Stay? You mean like a cell?"

"Yea, a room or something?" He knew the answer to the question, even as he asked it, the doom he felt was overwhelming.

"That's so cute," Lucifer said. "I think you know."

"Well," Mark's voice was shaking now, "Maybe tomorrow I could..."

Lucifer cut him off. "Tomorrow? There are no more tomorrows, Mark. This is your tomorrow. There is only NOW, and this is your reality, tomorrow is gone...now is all there is for you, and you will live here... in the now...forever."

The despair of it hit Mark hard and his knees buckled under him, he crumbled to the ground. The girls he had killed all came rushing back to him, he saw their faces...every one of them, and their eyes haunted him.

Lucifer turned and looked at Zuek and Imlack and said, "Welcome home, your pit awaits you."

He then turned to Azazel and said, "Take him." He pointed at the other Nephilim, "And find out where they went. You two come with me." He pointed at the two gatherers and walked away.

CHAPTER 18
Eye of The Hurricane

A great author once wrote, "There is something I do not know, the knowing of which, would change everything."

Amy and Johnathan have both reached a point in their lives when God has removed all the distractions, and has for a time, forced Himself into their lives. Oh the wonders of it all, the lengths and depths He will go to for them...for you.

As they finally reached the airport a storm was approaching the gulf. This was a big one, hurricane winds were clocking at a hundred and thirty miles an hour, and airports were closing all across the gulf coast. Miguel and Leahcim hurried to find a flight anywhere out of Louisiana towards the middle east or just out of Louisiana.

The last FedEx flight was leaving in a half hour, so Miguel, Leahcim, Pedro and Chewy cleared the flight of any demons. Leahcim using his third stone cast a spirit of deception to clear the flight and convince the crew that the guys were packages. *Two stones left*, he thought, *only two...* he worried.

As the plane lifted off the runway and into the night, lightning and thunder filled the sky.

The group all found reasonably comfortable places to sit and hang on, for what was to be, a very bumpy ride.

Johnathan was a bit like a puppy at this point and had found a new fondness for Amy. He found himself looking for any reason to be close to her.

Amy, although changed now, was still a little rough around the edges. Close to the texture of a cactus, but softening, she liked the idea of Johnathan's attempts to sit next to her. She wasn't sure about these new emotions she was having, she *needed* to keep her wit and sharp tongue! (Defenses and all that) They were new and a bit scary to her. She smiled at the effort Johnathan was making and as she looked over at him she saw past her contempt for him. *He's handsome*, she thought, *No! Why would he ... I mean I'm dead! ...Still pretty, but nonetheless dead...weird.* She leaned her head against a box and closed her eyes.

She started to think about the young girl, she had heard the girl's father on the phone, "As fast as I can honey!" A single tear rolled down her cheek.

Chewy touched her shoulder. He was standing in front of her holding out a Twinkie and smiling.

"Thank you Chewy." She said.

Chewy wiped the tear from her cheek and kissed her forehead. He liked the thought of her being happy about his food, he smiled and moved to the rest of the group, offering Twinkies and beef sticks.

The cargo hold of the plane was very loud and dimly lit. The roar of the engines made it difficult to talk, and the turbulence kept them bouncing around as the plane fought its way through the weather outside. The group hung on in silence, each in their own thoughts, examining all the recent events of the past few days.

As they half slept, and half braced themselves against all the bumps and sways, Johnathan suddenly felt something slam against his chest, nearly knocking the wind out of him.

He opened his eyes, there was a black mist floating a few feet away from him. Johnathan was sitting on a pile of boxes, and it charged again, hitting him so hard it knocked him clear off the boxes.

It growled at him, seeing Amy stir it whooshed toward her and slammed into her chest, she gasped, woke and screamed.

Leahcim stood up and yelled for Miguel. Chewy and Pedro moved from the back of the cargo hold and saw the Nephilim charging Amy. He was trying to enter and possess them but couldn't get in! He charged Amy a second time and she flew down the aisle of the aircraft from the impact. The demon backed away and hovered, facing them all. Before they could move in on him, he turned and went up the stairs to the upper deck of the plane.

As the group moved together, in the center of the cargo hold, the plane suddenly tilted uncontrollably in a hard nose dive. They were thrown to the front of the hold, smashed against the steel wall of the cargo hold and pinned against the fuselage. Trying to fight the gravity, they could feel the G-forces on their bodies as the plane rolled over and flew inverted while it continued to plummet. Taking the group with it as it rolled, they slammed against the ceiling of the plane.

Leahcim watched as his pouch detached from his belt... he reached for it right as the plane rolled again and threw them to the floor. Leahcim was frantically reaching for his pouch that had landed a few feet from him. It had spilled open, his stones and the manual were strewn all over the floor. They could hear the engines straining against the air outside, the plane began to shake, and it seemed as though it would break in half at any second. Just as quickly as it started, the plane leveled out and the engines returned to their normal hum. As if nothing had happened.

"WHAT THE HELL WAS THAT!?" The Captain was yelling at the co-pilot.

Buzzers and warning lights were sounding off all across the instrument panel, one by one they shut off as the plane righted itself and leveled.

"What the hell was that?" The Captain said again.

Air traffic control had seen the dive on radar. "Control to 1157 Fed, are you in distress?"

The Captain quickly responded, "1157 Fed, we're descending to five thousand and assessing, I'll get back with you."

"1157 Fed, clear to descend to five thousand."

"Roger."

Chewy was gathering his snacks and repacking them into his satchel, Amy and Johnathan were gathering themselves off the floor. Miguel, Leahcim and Pedro were in the center of the cargo.

"We cleared this plane!" Leahcim said as he gathered his stones off the floor. His manual had slipped under a crate just out of his sight.

Pedro nodded.

"He must have come in after we took off," Miguel replied.

Chewy had spotted a beef stick on top of one of the crates, so he climbed up on top of them and just as he reached across to get it, and his fingers were about to touch it, he was pulled violently over the crate and slammed to the floor. The Nephilim was on him, pinning him to the floor, fervently choking him, Chewy was struggling and kicking trying to break free. Miguel saw Chewy's feet disappear quickly over the crate and heard the struggle. As he bolted to help,

and he turned around the corner, the Nephilim hit Miguel at full speed, knocking him backward and into Pedro who was coming up behind him. It flew over the crates and headed for Johnathan, he slammed into him and threw him face first onto Amy and the two-landed hard against the metal floor. Everyone was scrambling to find their footing. The Nephilim disappeared again up the staircase to the upper deck.

"WE HAVE TO GET HIM!" Miguel shouted over the engines.

"HOW?" Leahcim yelled back.

Chewy was still behind the crates, huddled against the wall of the plane clutching his satchel. Pedro was kneeling beside him, he was motioning for Chewy to stay put and gave him the o.k. sign. He smiled at his friend and went to join the others.

Amy's heart was racing in her chest, Johnathan's eyes were wide, and his mind was racing. They both struggled to their feet, Johnathan was half bent over holding his back, breathing heavily.

"What do we do?" He shouted, looking at Leahcim.

The Captain was checking his gauges, the cockpit had suddenly become ice cold and he could see his own breath. He glanced over at his co-pilot and noticed he was rocking back and forth in his chair

"Allen?... Allen! .... ALLEN!" He shouted.

Allen turned his head toward the pilot... the Captain saw his eyes were black! His body began to convulse and shake, his head flew back against the headrest. Allen was resisting the demon, he began to shake uncontrollably as the demon struggled to stay inside.

Miguel turned to Pedro and said, "Find a blanket or sunthin we can throw over him, if we can cover it we can hold it! Vamonos!" He turned to Leahcim, "We have to trap it and hold him till we land!"

Pedro came back with a large packing blanket.

"This is good, Johnathan," he yelled. "Come stand by the staircase."

Johnathan moved into position near the bottom of the staircase.

"Ok, I'm going to make some noise and see if we can get him to come back, when he does jou turn and run towards the back. We'll get behind him and toss the blanket over him. Then everybody jumps on him, he's going to be very hard to handle but I thin we can do it, ok?"

They all nodded in agreement, and Leahcim headed for the cockpit.

Allen was holding both armrests of his chair, his fingers were locked onto them tightly. He was still convulsing and thrashing... and then suddenly he stopped. The demon heard a banging on the stairwell, and he left the cockpit abruptly. Allen slumped in his chair exhausted from the fight.

"Tower this is 1157 Fed requesting emergency landing, what's close?"

"1157 Fed, cleared for Marathon International. We'll clear the way."

Johnathan looked up the stairwell, he saw the demon as it hovered at the top, growling. Johnathan's heart was pounding, "Oh," he muttered nervously before turning and bolting down the aisle. As he reached the end of the fuselage he tripped, and the demon flew right past him and out the back of the plane. Johnathan slid into a crate with a crash, then sat halfway up and looked back at the others. He shrugged and shook his head, standing up he said, "Well that was easy!"

The demon screeched as it re-entered the rear of the plane with full velocity and slammed into Johnathan, sending him back down the aisle. He slid until he hit Pedro's legs, knocking him into Amy, who then toppled and landed on top of Johnathan. The demon whooshed down the aisle screaming as it came upon Miguel who held open the blanket, it slammed into him knocking him backward onto the staircase. He closed his arms tightly around the demon and held on, the demon flew to the top of the fuselage, hitting Miguel's head against the ceiling and back down to the floor. Miguel held on tight as the demon roared down the aisle and slammed into the crates at the other end. He was up again and slammed against the side of the fuselage, Miguel lost his grip the demon turned and flew out the rear of the plane.

Miguel slumped down, catching his breath. The others rushed to the rear of the plane.

"He's gone," Amy said.

They all heard the ear-piercing scream from outside the plane.

"What's that?' Amy asked.

Johnathan braced himself for another impact.

"It's him," Miguel replied. "He's calling the others." Miguel stood up and leaned towards the side of the plane listening.

It was screaming over and over.

"We have to leave!" Miguel shouted, "NOW!"

"Leave?" Amy and Johnathan yelled at the same time. "How are we gonna leave if we're thirty thousand feet in the air!?" Johnathan said, incredulously.

"Jor going to jump, come on." Miguel moved towards the rear cargo door.

"I'm not going anywhere!" Amy shouted.

We're landing in Marathon, Florida. We'll have to come in low over the water, we can do this!"

"No! No way! No, I'm **not** jumping!" Amy said, shaking her head vigorously.

"LISTIN TO ME! THIS PLANE WILL BE FULL OF DEMONS ANY MINUTE NOW, JOU MUST JUMP!!"

The demon continued to scream outside the plane.

"Jou gotta jump! Jou're already dead, sort of. It won't hurt and jou'll land in the water...hopefully."

"Hopefully? Hopefully!?" She yelled.

"Amy," Leahcim said, "I'll be with you all the way! He's right you shouldn't feel a thing!"

"Shouldn't?? Shouldn't?!" She was looking at all three of them, eyes wide in panic.

"Send him first!" She pointed at Johnathan.

"Oh yea, she's changed. A whole new girl." Johnathan quipped.

Miguel pushed the emergency lever opening the cargo doors, the air rushed in and took their breath away. The runway lights were approaching fast.

"I'M NOT REA..," Amy started, as Miguel pushed Amy out the door.

Leahcim jumped...Then Johnathan...Chewy, beef stick half opened hanging from his mouth, his satchel close to his chest, closed his eyes and jumped. They were one mile off the coast of Florida and a hundred and fifty feet in the air when they jumped.

Miguel and Pedro backed up the aisle as the demon slid along the outside of the plane, they watched as he peered around the doorway and entered the plane, they could see more coming in the distance...

CHAPTER 19
Trickery

    Lucifer was again in his office laying on his couch, a bag of Cheetos in one hand and a remote in the other, channel surfing. News... the puppy channel... infomercial... the cat channel.... more news... ah televangelism! He loved these! Many of these guys were his protégés, he had been working and grooming them for years. A lot of them started out with the truth but being who he was and true to his nature, he had managed to work in the deceit. A little compromise here, a little there, it wasn't hard to get these guys headed in the right direction. Then at the right moment some cash always seemed to do the trick. Once they saw the money begin to flow, well... that was their weakness.

    This one was saying, "Listen friends I'm gonna let you in on one of God's great promises... if you'll send a gift of a hundred dollars or five hundred dollars, God is going to send you a hundred-fold what you send us!"

    Lucifer laughed out loud. "These monkeys crack me up, they believe it too!"

    "That's right friends! A gift today of five hundred and God's gonna turn that into fifty thousand! It's the miracle of giving, a hundred-fold, that's what His word says! You show God your willingness to believe His promises and He will bless you beyond your wildest dreams!"

    Lucifer loved this because when the "promise" didn't show up, it caused so many to lose faith, and lost faith was his chief objective with believers.

    "These monkeys are so desperate," he was talking to the television, "they never stop to think maybe the preacher should send them five hundred bucks! IDIOTS! Ah... the love of money, truly the root of all my fun!"

He turned off the television and picked up his bible... Yes, Lucifer reads his bible, mostly the new testament. He was always searching for a loophole, something God missed, something he could use. It gave him a headache though all this hope and love, it was gross. The old testament was just a reminder of past mistakes, he didn't know God would use his past to plot his future. There had to be a mistake somewhere, it was all written out right here.

"Why would God show me the plan?" He had pondered this for thousands of years. "It's here, I know it's here!" He was quite obsessed with it.

He went and stood in front of the mirror and looked at himself. He began changing body types, turning from one image into another... his mist self, black and flowing with the air in the room. Then an angel of light, white robe, dark hair, flaming sword. Then a small Jewish man (one of his favorites) Kippa, robe, beard. Then, to his own surprise, the angel he was *before* the fall.

Lucifer stared at the image in the mirror... he was handsome, gallant, truly God's best.

He looked at the image up and down, he turned sideways looking over his shoulder, "His favorite," he mumbled. He turned to face the image head on, and his form faded and turned into a pale ghostly image, with grey skin and protruding cheek bones. He now had long ears and a hairless body, rotting teeth with drool coming from the corner of his mouth. His wings no longer held feathers, just rotting flesh. And immediately, he went black... back to his mist.

He moved back to his couch, flopped down and tried to make his headache go away. His mind drifted to Zuek, *That little rat fink!*, he thought. He went over the thoughts and images he had seen in Zuek's mind. *Johnathan,* he thought, *oh I hate these humans!*

He wanted to concentrate on Johnathan, but his mind kept pulling him back to Zuek's words. "Lucifer you fool...," it made him feel sick to his stomach. He wasn't the fool he thought.

"The Son was the fool!" He said out loud. "I wouldn't take a single lash for these humans!" He remembered a million angels, at least, he saw their white robes, their swords and horses and chariots. He remembered their silence... smiling under their solemn faces. He pushed the thought of them laughing to themselves out of his mind.

He thought of all the time he had spent on the Pharisees, *they had played so easily into my hands, and that puke of a disciple...what was his name?...Judas! A good example of how money can make friends and influence people!*

His plan was a good one, creation killing the creator! It was awesome, the greatest insult. He had spent thirty years watching, plotting, and planting seeds of doubt and deceit. *Man that would have been perfect!*, he thought. It had crossed his mind at one point, during the walk to Golgotha, but he had brushed it off, he was already committed, and everyone was there... and there was no way God was going to hang his son from a cross, not for those humans no way! He remembered the feeling of the blood rushing from his face. Oh how he hated that day! And then the ultimate insult, He wrote a book (after the fact of course) about the whole plan, redemption, and sacrifice, all of it!

"Trickery, deceit, lies!!" He shouted out loud. "He can lie, deceive and fool, but I try it and I'm the father of ALL lies! The whole world stops turning! Not fair!" He was a mist now, hugging the ceiling of his office, just floating there. He flew down to the mirror again.

"HE LOVED ME BEST! I WAS HIS FAVORITE!" He yelled as he changed to his former angelic being again...he looked so good. "AAGGHH!" He turned away from the mirror.

He receded deep into the memory... He remembered the groan he heard, a slow deep moan from within the earth as The Son's first drop of blood hit the ground. He had looked down at the stain on the ground and then up into Zuek's eyes... he had heard it too... he remembered the feeling growing in his stomach, and the words echoed in his ears.

"Eloi Eloi lama sabachthani!" (My God, my God why have you forsaken me!) He suddenly felt very sick and very small as he looked up at the cross, the rain hitting him in the eyes. It seemed so big... as if it reached all the way to heaven, and then he heard the Son say "TETELESTAI" (Paid in full). The body of the Son hung there, his head down blood spilling from his side. It was as if the rain and blood were cleansing the whole earth... he stumbled backward still looking up, the earth was shaking violently...

Paid in full. Lucifer sat down on the edge of his couch and shook his head looking at the floor. "Tetelestai," he said softly under his breath.

Looking back at four thousand maybe five thousand years, he could see the set up. It was obvious now, and of course there's the book now too. He was not going to fold and give up. After Golgotha he had changed plans, regrouped as it were. If he couldn't stop redemption, if he couldn't change God's mind about these rats, then he could mess with their faith or better yet, keep them from coming at all. The ones he could keep for himself he could build an army with, he'd read the book and he knew how it was supposed to end.

This current event with this chubby oaf of an angel could play well into his overall plan. He couldn't help but wonder, *What in heaven would change if I were to kill this chubby little rat? Will it all unravel like a cheap suit? Will the universe split open or collapse on itself? If God truly made a mistake that means, it's all a farce and subject to who knows what!* Lucifer had absolutely nothing to lose.

"I mean what's the worst that could happen," he said out loud, "I suddenly don't exist? It all implodes? Phhhft. So what!"

He had made up his mind, he would grab the chubby little guy, ask for a ransom meeting, and insist God and his family be there and just as they agree to his terms...run a sword through the angel. And let what happens happen. "My own Tetelestai." He said to the empty room.

As he sat, years of memories came flooding back. Every time he got a foothold somewhere, God seemed to be one step ahead of him, and it would blow up in his face. It seemed to him the only success he had was with these monkeys that God loved. He had millions of them, in the pit you couldn't swing a stick without hitting dozens, and the pit was huge! *What if,* he thought, *What if this is a trick too, what if the souls I have aren't real? What if God created some humans for destruction, or 'throw aways'? It makes sense in that the ones who believe are already His, pre-destined... and the others are just...empty shells... that's how God won't lose any. What if...,* he thought *this is all for the benefit of the believers? To grow them and teach them, to mold them into HIS image. He's creating the perfect, free willed, God taught, manicured beings.*

"Oh crap! He's gonna fill heaven with these, he's gonna have them judge the angels!"

It was all coming together now. His only hope now was to kill the angel and unravel this whole mess, or else the book would end as it had been written, and he was gonna burn.

Leahcim was... ironically... his salvation...or so it seemed.

CHAPTER 20
Who Is This Guy... Really?

Azazel and his hounds had tracked the group to a gas station in a small town in Louisiana. They arrived as the events were unfolding in the parking lot, he held back his hounds and stood off at a distance and watched. Azazel's attention was drawn not to the shooting but to Miguel. He watched as everyone one else was in a frantic scramble to save the girl, but Miguel, rather than fight, stood straight up, spread out his arms and looked up to heaven and closed his eyes.

Then Azazel saw it! An angel appeared briefly, just long enough to stop the bullets from Mark's gun and was gone.

He had called forth an angel! But how? Who on earth can call forth an angel? Azazel's mind was scrambling for an answer. He had seen Miguel at Sodom and knew he was connected to heaven... but this was so much more. As he continued to watch, he saw the two demons take Johnathan, and he also saw an opportunity to get Leahcim. Instead, he decided to follow the demons and take Johnathan if Lucifer didn't pick up on this.

Azazel left his hounds outside the barn as he slipped in unnoticed and hovered near the ceiling. He was listening, waiting for an opportunity. He still had an uneasy feeling about Miguel that he couldn't shake. He listened to Imlack and Zuek as they planned their next moves and watched as Imlack left on his assignment. Then he listened as Johnathan questioned Zuek.

As Zuek recounted the events at Golgotha, Azazel's mind went back, he remembered that day as well. He remembered the army of God and the vast number of angels and it sparked another memory, a similar event when hundreds of thousands of God's army ruined what appeared to be certain victory...

~ 150 ~

He was working on the Arameans to take Israel. He had worked for so long and spent hundreds of hours on this idiot, and he had finally convinced the King to invade and capture the land. He was about to strike... and he remembered... Elisha! This prophet of God kept interrupting Azazel's plans, telling the King of Israel what they were doing. So, he had convinced the king to go and kill Elisha! Azazel found him in Dothan a small city outside of Shechem. They had surrounded the city with a large army, with soldiers, horses and chariots, Azazel remembered standing in the gateway of the city ready to strike.

As the commander was about to give the order they heard the thundering of horse hooves and chariots, he turned and saw thousands and thousands of soldiers, all in white and chariots with wheels on fire! Archers and sword wielding warriors of God, they were everywhere! Now they were surrounded, as they turned to fight these soldiers of God... his humans were struck blind! He couldn't believe this! A hundred thousand **blind** soldiers with one word from this prophet! He watched in disbelief as the prophet told them 'They weren't who they were looking for, nor were they even in the right city' then he led his great army away and into the hands of the Samarians! Azazel stood mouth open and watched as his henchmen just wander off behind Elisha like stupid sheep!

He turned to the army of God, he looked across the hillside that was covered in white robed men, dancing horses eager to run into battle, and chariots with wheels still ablaze. He caught the eyes of one of the soldiers on horseback. He seemed to be at the front of the great army, his horse was raring up underneath him, dancing from side to side, and then this soldier did something strange. He spread his arms, put his head back and closed his eyes... just like Miguel had done in the parking lot! And the army just turned and disappeared.

Azazel's head was spinning as the memories of a hundred other battles raced through his head. He thought of Gideon and how three hundred men, dog lapping men, had defeated another great protégé of his...*Valiant warrior! Gimme a break! He was a farm boy, never fought a single battle,* he thought. He had a sneaking suspicion Miguel was involved in that one as well.

He listened as Zuek went on, watching as he slammed his fist against the stall door and stormed out. He saw Johnathan hit his knees and scream at God. Azazel had seen this before, it was usually the beginning of the end for an undecided. He was turning and not in a good direction, but toward God. He had to move fast and get him now or it may be too late!

He watched Johnathan lay down and fall into a dream. Azazel wanted to see this, he could learn who the players were in a human's life by watching dreams. Angels, God, and Lucifer would often reveal themselves in the subconscious, in dreams.

Water, uh-oh already a bad sign. It usually meant the Holy Spirit was there. He was in a boat with no motor and no oars... drifting signified lost. Then Lucifer, he was playing the same old trick, get them to reach out to him and take his hand not God's. He watched as Lucifer manipulated the dream... and he saw another man appear in the distance out on the water, standing.

"Oh crap, that's not good." Azazel said under his breath. "Joshua or whatever name he's using today." Then the chubby angel on the other side of the boat quoting scripture and pointing. He could tell Johnathan didn't understand the man on the water, he didn't recognize him yet, but Azazel knew it meant he didn't have long.

Joshua, he thought, *Rescuer. Why doesn't he just tell these monkeys who he is and be done with it? Save us all a lot of time!* His thoughts were interrupted when he heard the familiar snapping sound of the stone being cast and saw the Amber colored light as it drifted across the field.

Azazel headed for the clouds as high as he could go, he watched as the light from the stone made its way across the field hitting its targets as it went. He watched as Miguel and the others left the gas station and made it to the farm. He waited for the light to dissipate and then moved back down to the barn. As he entered the barn he heard Lucifer, still in the dream, yell out Zuek's name. He had found Zuek, he didn't have much time. Amy entered the barn and snuck up behind Zuek smacking him hard with a shovel in the back of the head. Azazel felt Lucifer's presence getting close, so he grabbed one of his fellow Nephilim and said, "Follow them."

He scattered his hounds, still confused they just wandered off into the field mumbling and slapping each other on the back of the head, some vomiting from the smell of nearby humans.

As Lucifer approached, Azazel gathered Imlack from the field and brought him to the barn. The two met at the entrance to the barn.

"Were have you been?" Lucifer hissed.

"Tracking your friends," Azazel replied as he pointed to Imlack and Zuek. "These two had other plans for them, it seems you have some dissention to deal with." Azazel smirked.

"Grass is always deader on the other side," Lucifer replied.

Before long the two were in the pit, Azazel hadn't been there in years. He had forgotten how warm it was, he hadn't been this warm in a long time. As Lucifer dealt with the new arrival and the two traitors, Azazel moved around the pit just to re-familiarize himself with it.

He remembered the holes that were all over the place, they were like fox holes in the military, but these were dug by souls looking for a place that wasn't so hot. He could see thousands of them, with just the tops of heads protruding out. The great chasms that would spit fire, offering cool pools of water just on the other side of the great gap.

Tens of thousands would stand and gaze across, for many the need for water was just too tempting and they would plummet into who knows where trying to make the leap. The screams are what he remembered most, not too loud but always screaming in the distance...

just out of view. It was the screaming that eventually sent him out into the cold. As he walked he saw many of his past possessions, ones he recognized from his time on earth. They made him smile, their misery, he loved the look of absolute despair on their faces. He knew some of them recognized him as well, he could see it in their eyes, that look of seeing the one who deceived them was priceless. They wanted to attack him, they wanted to kill him, but they retreated into their despair knowing it was useless. *They were pathetic in life and even more so in their death!* He thought.

He found himself at the old holding area, it was where they used to bring new souls, before the Son had ruined everything. A large flat rock that protruded out over a huge gulf that was filled with fire, and on the other side of the gulf was a beautiful grassy meadow. A beam of sunshine hit the meadow where Father Abraham used to sit and comfort the recently dead believers. He would clean their wounds and give them water from the small stream that ran through the meadow. It was absolute torture for new souls in hell, almost too cruel he thought. Nah, he wished they would bring it back!

He considered Lucifer's plan to enlist all these souls into his army for the final battle against God and His army. It was a sound plan, millions of very angry people fighting to get out of here, it would be one heck of a fight!

He also considered Zuek's current predicament, he had planned against Lucifer and was found out and would now be confined to whatever size hole he could dig to escape the heat. Azazel gazed across at the meadow...he and Zuek may be able to help each other.

Azazel's thoughts were broken by screaming from one of his soldiers, a long way away, faint, far off, they had found them!

CHAPTER 21
The Second Fall

SCREAMING! FALLING! SCREAMING! FALLING! MORE SCREAMING! MORE FALLING!

Amy hit the water and skipped across it like a stone, coming to rest in about two feet of water right at the edge of the island.

"Oh... Oh God!" She said terrified, her heart feeling like it would explode. "Oh, am I dead? Again?" She laid there afraid to move. Jonathan bounced across the water as well, he hit the beach feet first and flew across the sand and landed on his face. Leahcim just kind of slid in as if he had done this a thousand times before. Chewy however, well Chewy hit and sunk like a rock.

Johnathan rolled over and shouted, "That...was...so cool! Oh man, that was awesome!"

Amy, laying on her back, still afraid to move, just groaned. She just knew something had to be broken, or she was terribly maimed in some horrific way. She lifted her head and examined her body. She seemed ok. She saw Chewy pop up from under the water, and he held up his satchel and smiled, giving her the thumbs up. The food was safe!

Leahcim, stood up and scanned the area for demons or Nephilim. The hurricane was just coming ashore, the authorities had evacuated the island as a precaution. Heavy rains and horrific winds were pounding the island... it was empty, no people, no demons, they were alone.

Johnathan looked at Leahcim and asked, "What now?"

"Let's move into one of those." He pointed to a brick and stucco cabana, they were built to weather the worst storms and should provide reasonably safe shelter.

They gathered themselves and pulled Chewy from the water and made their way into one of the cabanas. The wind was howling outside, and it was now raining in sheets. This had been an incredibly exhausting few hours. Amy, as usual headed straight for the shower. Chewy sat on the living room floor and emptied his satchel onto the floor, scanning to see what, if any of their food he could salvage. Leahcim pulled towels from the hallway and began passing them out while Johnathan searched for flashlights and candles.

Amy stood in the bathroom and stared in the mirror, and she realized her knees were still shaking. Her makeup was everywhere except where she had applied it. She crumbled to the floor in a ball, she was in shock. She had died in a violent car crash, been attacked by so many creepers that she couldn't even keep track. She'd witnessed a kidnapper trying to abduct a girl, she'd been involved in a shootout with police and had then been thrown out of an airplane! She laid there trembling, thinking she just wanted this to end! When would it end?!

Johnathan on the other hand was all charged up. This was such the opposite of his normal life, he loved the jump from the plane. He was ready for anything he thought. He was amped!

He gathered candles and flash lights and brought them to the living room and sat down with Leahcim and Chewy.

"You think we'll be safe here?" He asked Leahcim.

"Well, we're safer here in a hurricane than out there," he replied.

"Won't they look for shelter too?"

"No, this weather doesn't bother them, anything is better than the pit. They love this stuff, you know just a different kind of mayhem for them."

"Oh right," Johnathan said.

Chewy was surrounded by snacks, all laid out in a circle around him. He was smiling, nothing was ruined apart from one opened, half eaten, soggy Twinkie. He shook his head almost in grief for the Twinkie.

Amy came out of the bathroom wrapped in a fluffy white hotel robe and flopped down on the couch with a heavy but relieved sigh. Chewy moved across the floor on his knees and presented her with Two Twinkies and a beef stick and a giant smile.

"Thank you Chewy," she said with a smile.

Chewy's heart leapt at the thought of his food making her happy. He turned and handed out food to Leahcim and Johnathan.

"What about Miguel and Pedro? Do you think they're alright?" Amy asked looking at everyone.

Chewy looked at the group and smiled nodding his head yes.

"They've been fighters for a long time," Leahcim said. "We're close to the airport, I think they'll find us once they dispatch the Nephilim."

"What if they don't? I mean...," She glanced at Chewy. "What if they lose?" she whispered.

Chewy shook his head and frowned at her.

"Let's see what morning brings." Leahcim said gently.

As they settled in, they lit candles and listened to the wind and rain howling outside the door. Johnathan sat on the end of the couch opposite Amy, his feet stretched out on the coffee table, and his arms behind his head.

"I still don't understand this," he said to Leahcim.

"Which part?" Leahcim asked.

"All of it really." Johnathan replied. "I mean, if God wants us all to come to Him then why not just show Himself? Just show up and say, 'Here I am, I'm God and you're not. Follow me.'
I mean, it seems to me, that He could have saved a lot of time and trouble. Then everyone would believe and we would all live happily ever after, right?"

"Not everyone who believes, wants to be with Him." Leahcim said.

"What? How is that possible? If they believe in Him they automatically go? I mean to heaven, right? That's what you said."

"Yea, but some believe He exists they just don't want to be like him. They want to be like the world, they want the things the world offers them, darker things."

"So, you're saying some people believe, but choose not to go?"

"When Adam and Eve where presented with a choice, it was designed to be that way.
God knew they would be tempted, and he knew what the outcome would be. He also knew that every human born from Adam and Eve would now be contaminated, no longer pure, no longer of Him. Now they would have to choose, each and every one would have to make their own choice. Good or evil, cursing or blessing, love Him or not." Leahcim paused for a moment.

"To answer your question specifically, some would rather live their lives doing whatever *they* want, however they choose, with no rules, and God allows that. It's your choice and yours alone."

"It doesn't seem fair. I mean, what if I never wanted to be born, or to exist, but He created me anyway and now I'm forced to choose, and I don't want to choose." Johnathan retorted.

"What if I told you that that thought process is situational?" Leahcim replied.

"What do you mean?"

"God's ways are not your ways, His thoughts are not your thoughts, His thoughts and ways are so much higher than yours, that the rational you just used is indicative of a bad situation. No money, no job, no love in your life, it's depression basically. And what if I told you that God, knowing *all* of these thoughts and feelings that you're experiencing, still knew, that this situation would draw you closer to Him? He allowed this situation in your life at this very time, and also knowing, that in the end, you would come to Him as one of his children. A child who he has known and loved since before you were created in the womb."

Leahcim continued, "Fairness Johnathan, is having allowed that situation in your life with the foreknowledge of where it would lead you and walking with you, through it all. Even while you cuss and blame Him, and kick and scream, He never leaves your side. He has infinite patience. And just so you know, He knows your name Johnathan – it is written on the palm of His hand. In the end when you come to Him, and He spends the rest of your life teaching you and guiding you, walking by your side, you'll understand. You'll understand that this life is a gift, this thing you 'don't want to choose' is irreplaceable and sacred. Today, you hate every minute of it, but tomorrow when you discover His abundant love, that's waiting for you, you'll realize that He has brought you here with the sole hope that you would choose to believe in Him."

Amy sat quietly looking at the floor, a tear running down her cheek, looked at Leahcim and said softly, "I believe."

"I know," Leahcim replied and smiled.

Chewy interrupted, tapping Johnathan's shoulder.

"What?" Johnathan asked.

Chewy made a heart shape with his hands and pointed up nodding.

"Yes," Johnathan said.

Chewy took a pad and pen and scribbled something and handed it to Johnathan. It read 'Kitchen, more food.' With a smiley face, Chewy pointed at the door.

"Yea I guess so."

"What's it say?" Leahcim asked.

"He wants to go to the main hotel kitchen and get food."

"I'm in," Amy said. "I'd love something real to eat."

"Should be alright, I think all the demons followed the people out of here." Leahcim said.

With that the three found rain ponchos and umbrellas and left the bungalow.

Chewy got way out ahead of Amy and Johnathan, they were surprised by how fast the chubby little Mexican could move. They ran across the grounds of the hotel, dodging puddles and fallen tree limbs. As they came to a fallen palm tree, Johnathan crossed first and then reached out for Amy's hand to help her cross. Her heart skipped a little, she took his hand and was quite pleased when he didn't let go of it as they continued running through the rain.

"Wait," Amy shouted. She had lost a shoe in a mud puddle. "My shoe!" Johnathan got down on his knees and searched the muddy water, as Amy leaned against a palm tree. A gust of wind took Amy's umbrella ripping it from her hands.

"Got it!" Johnathan yelled over the wind.

He crawled over on his knees to where Amy was leaning against the tree. He took her foot in his hand and slid the shoe back on her foot. He raised himself up and found himself face to face with Amy. His knees were shaking, and his heart pounded as he looked into her beautiful blue eyes.

Amy's mind was in full race mode as she found herself staring into Johnathan's hazel eyes. Her heart was pounding in her chest, and the rain was pounding their faces. For what seemed like an eternity they looked at one another. Then slowly, Johnathan leaned in and kissed her. The rain poured down on them, but they were oblivious. He kissed her like his life depended on it, and time stood still. When he finally pulled back, she whispered breathlessly, "Wow."

Something happened to both of them in that kiss. Years of this weird thing that was between them, this thing that neither would let come forward, just evaporated. Everything they had both thought of so briefly, but would push away, all came out in that one kiss. He leaned in and kissed her again, softly, as if he had waited to taste her lips his whole life. He held both her hands in his, staring at her.

"Maybe we should go find the kiss...I mean the food. Kisses and the food, I mean Chewy and the food," Amy stammered. Her head was spinning. She looked at Johnathan and then turned to run toward the hotel, but instead ran head first into another tree, and fell flat on her rear.

Johnathan picked her up and they made their way to the hotel lobby, holding hands as they ran. Inside, the lobby was dimly lit by the emergency generators. They could hear Chewy as he rattled pots and pans in the kitchen. They found him with his head inside one of the refrigerators, humming happily. He turned and smiled widely, placing a ham inside his satchel. He frowned as he discovered it wouldn't fit. Amy found a large box and handed it to Chewy, his eyes lit up.

"There ya go buddy," she said.

Suddenly the air was pierced with what sounded like a howl mixed with a shriek. It was a terrifying sound that sent a chill down everyone's spines.

"What was that?" Johnathan said as he looked at the others. It happened again, and the three looked at each other, Chewy's eyes widened, he picked up his satchel and held it to his chest. It came again, this time a second howl followed by a short scream from a different direction. They could tell there were two of them...outside in the lobby area.

"Night screamers."

Amy and Johnathan both jumped and let out a scream.

"Oh God," Amy cried as she held her heart.

They turned to see an elderly looking black man, dressed in a security guard uniform.

"They're night screamers," He said again.

"Who are you? Wait, you can see us?" Johnathan said, confused.

"Name's Zib, and yes I can see you. I was told you'd be coming."

"Who told you we'd be coming?"

"Not important, what is important is to get away from those night screamers. Where are you guys hiding?"

"Over in one of the cabanas," Johnathan replied.

"Alright, out the back door. Let's go." Zib pointed to the back entrance.

As they made their way back to the cabana they could hear the night screamers howling back and forth to each other.

"What's a night screamer?" Amy asked.

"Just another demon," Zib answered. "They **are** the things that go bump in the night. Lucifer uses them to invade dreams. They're the things nightmares are made of, or should I say they *make* the nightmares."

"Will they find us?" Johnathan said.

"They haven't yet." Zib replied. "They're just hunting right now, they haven't seen you yet."

The rain had stopped for the time being, and they made their way through the darkness toward the cabana. Zib suddenly stopped and held out his arm to slow the others, lightening lit up the night, and up ahead, in the skyline standing on the horizon, they could make out two figures standing in the trees.

"Who are they?" Johnathan asked intrepidly, as he put his arm around Amy's waist and pushed her behind him. The two figures disappeared into the darkness.

"I don't know," Zib answered "Not demons."

Chewy, was still clutching his satchel and balancing a box full of ham. He tapped Zib's arm and pointed toward the cabana, it was just to the right of where they had seen the two figures.

"Alright, let's go around to the other side." Zib instructed. Another crack of lightning lit up the night as they turned. "AGHH!" Johnathan and Amy screamed at the same time.

"Jou are afraid of the dark, my Jewish friend?"

"Miguel!" Amy shouted, and she ran and threw her arms around him.

He and Pedro were standing there smiling, Chewy dropped his ham and satchel and grabbed Pedro in a bear hug. He reached over and pulled Miguel into the rather long reunion and kissing of cheeks that ensued.

Johnathan stood staring at Miguel who was now dressed in a brown robe with red and white stripes running through it. His mind shot back to his dream on the water.

"Nice robe." Amy said.

"Jou like it? It's not too much? I thin it makes me look thinner, don't jou?" He said, turning from side to side.

"Very thin and very handsome!" Amy answered. She looked at Pedro who was still fighting off Chewy and his cheek kissing.

"And look at you!" Pedro was wearing a moo-moo, bright colored and way too big, blue and green flowers all over it. He blushed and shrugged.

"What happened?" Amy asked.

"Oh jou should have seen it! The plane was overrun by fire crews and cops, it was crazy. They started spraying foam and water all over the place. The Nephilim took off before we could fight! Cowards! The ambulance guys felt sorry for us, and they gave us the clothes. I thin Pedro looks cute though, that's a good look for him!" Pedro blushed again, and shook his head no.

Johnathan watched in awe at the sight of Miguel, in the robe. He couldn't shake the feeling.

It can't be him, he thought.

Amy interrupted his thought, "Are you ok? You look funny."

"No, I'm ok." He answered, still looking at Miguel. He turned to Amy and smiled.

Miguel looked over Johnathan and Amy's shoulders, "Bangla? Pedro, LOOK! IT'S ZIB!" Chewy smiled and nodded his head yes.

"Hello Miguel."

"Oh, jou came! This makes me very pleased! WHERE HAVE JOU BEEN?" Miguel moved past Johnathan and Amy, and hugged Zib, slapping him on the back.

"You know, fighting the good fight." Zib replied.

"And jor so black! Look at jou!" Miguel said, as he pushed Zib back, holding both his arms and looking him up and down.

"Now, I've always been black. Suddenly you have a problem with that, maybe you should ask Miriam how that turned out for her!" Zib said raising an eyebrow.

Miguel turned to Amy and Johnathan and said, "He's very touchy about dis. I like to pick on him." Miguel continued, "Miriam was Moses' sister. Moses took a black woman from Ethiopia as his wife, but Miriam didn't like this, she make such a fuss over the issue that God took notice. The Father does not know race or color, just the heart. Anyway, to teach her and all of jou, He gave her leprosy, she turned white as snow! She was the original cracker!" He laughed at his own joke.

"What happened to her?" Amy asked.

As he was laughing, he said, "Oh cracker, that was a good one, jes?" Chewy smiled and nodded. "She saw how God felt about this and understood he has no concern with skin, only heart, and she repented and was healed."

Miguel laughed and hugged Zib again, "I have missed jou!"

As they entered the cabana, Leahcim stood up and smiled as he heard Miguel's voice and the others.

"Look who we found!" Miguel said excitedly.

"BANGLA!" Leahcim shouted.

"Zib found our friends in the kitchen," Miguel said.

"Yes, surrounded by screamers," Zib said.

"And where did they find you?" Leahcim asked looking at Miguel.

"Lost in the trees, looking for jous."

"Did you say Jews?" Zib asked.

"Oh man, here we go again!" Johnathan said.

They all laughed. Zib looked at Johnathan and said, "It's ok kid, you're in a room full of old Jews, black, brown, and white you just don't know it yet."

Miguel changed the subject, "Chewy what's for dinner?"

CHAPTER 22
The Book

As the fire crew filled the cabin of the plane with foam, Azazel and his soldiers watched as Miguel and Pedro were taken away and put in an ambulance. As the foam reached the door and started to spread out, Azazel spotted a book floating in the foam. He picked it up, read the cover and turned to his soldiers and said, "Pull everyone out of Syria! Wait for me in the caves near the dead sea."

Azazel made his way back to the pit, he found the hottest rock he could and sat down to read. He glanced over every page.

"We never had a manual," he said out loud. "So many secrets!" He reached the last chapter What To Do If You're Trapped On Earth. "The gate! They're going to the old gate!" He walked over and grabbed Zuek by the crown of his head, pulled him out of his hole and sat him on the rock next to him.

"The eye of the needle, where is it?" Azazel had never spent any time in the old city. During the years before the Son's arrival he spent all of his time possessing and fighting against Israel and its kings.

"Take me with you and I'll show you," Zuek answered. "You want a body, I want out of here forever, the humans are our tickets, take me with you!"

Azazel took Zuek to the great chasm, that before the Son, was used for new souls. He looked across at the meadow and the brook and said, "What do you see?"

"Abraham's bosom." Zuek answered.

"I see a new home. I see water, I see warmth." He looked at one of the souls walking by, "I see a permanent body." Azazel tore out the last chapter of the book and held the remainder of the book out over the fire, scorching the edges. As it caught fire he blew it out. "Go back to your hole, I'll be back for you in a day or two, be ready."

Azazel left the caverns and headed to Lucifer's office, and Zuek went back to his hole. Imlack raised his eyes from his hole a few feet from where Azazel had sat reading... out loud.

Lucifer was walking up the aisle of Walmart with the two gatherers, he paused, picking up a paint brush. "You two did a good job with Mark, really nice work." He continued walking, then stopped and picked up a plastic tarp and handed it to one of the demons. The demons smiled at each other.

"I smell promotion," one said as he slapped the other on the back of the head.

"Promotion? Oh, much more than that." Lucifer said as he picked out a box cutter.

"Are we painting your office sir?" the demon asked.

"Yes, we are." Lucifer answered.

"What color?"

"Puke green"

"Oh I like that," the other demon said.

As they entered Lucifer's office, he turned to them gesturing toward the tarp in the demons hand, "Help me spread this out," he said.

They spread the tarp out under a large wall.

"Come over here," he positioned the first demon on top of the tarp next to the wall.

"We forgot the paint." The demon said.

"No, it's right here." Lucifer took the box cutter and slashed the demons stomach, green slime gushed from the wound.

"You two morons were just twenty feet away from my prize!" The demon gasped and fell to his knees, spilling green slime into a puddle next to his body. He walked over to the other demon and took the paint brush from his trembling hand.

"TWENTY FEET! Instead of an ANGEL, you brought me a PEDOPHILE!" He reached down and began to soak up the slime from the demon with the paint brush. "HELL IS FILLED WITH PEDOPHILES!" He yelled. He began to paint, he was spelling out a name on the wall.

"You know what we don't have in hell?" He asked as he dipped his brush again.

The demon shook his head, watching as Lucifer finished the name.

"HIM! WE DON'T HAVE HIM!" The name was in large capital letters...LEAHCIM!!!

"How is it that this world is filled with demons, I mean you can't swing a dead cat without hitting sixteen of you idiots, and yet, this fat angel and two idiots just slip through your hands!? I don't get it! Pick that up," he motioned to the bleeding demon, "AND GO FIND HIM!"

The demon wrapped the tarp around his fallen friend, and hurriedly left the room, dragging the tarp out the door. Lucifer flopped down in his chair and put his head in his hands and stared at the name on the wall.

He started thinking of this group of mistakes he was chasing, *Leahcim*, he thought.

Johnathan, Amy, the two dirty Mexicans and their leader, what was his name...Miguel! As he was thinking Azazel appeared at his door.

"What?"

"I think you're gonna like this." He threw the book on Lucifer's desk.

"What is this?" Lucifer asked huffily.

"Training manual for angels." Azazel replied proudly.

"Where did you get this? We never had manuals!" Lucifer exclaimed.

"The little angel must have dropped it. We found it on the plane."

"YA KNOW, YOU MIGHT WANT TO SHARE SOME OF THESE DETAILS WITH ME! WHAT PLANE?"

Azazel explained what had happened, and how he found the book. He left out the part about Zuek, and he lied and said he found the book in the fire on the plane, and that just as it was burning he saw the words, Get To Rome.

He surmised that it only made sense that the trapped angel would have to get to Rome, to the Vatican to make it out safely.

"Well then," Lucifer started, "Let's let them get to Rome." As he said that, a shriek came from his office doorway that made Lucifer jump and turn. Looking at the screamer standing there he said, "Geeze! You guys need to learn how to communicate better! What do you want!?"

"We found them, they're in a hotel in Florida!"

"All of them, they're still together?"

"Yes sir, there's seven of them."

"Seven? Who else is with them?"

"The angel, the two humans, the hell hounders, and a black guy named Nib... or Bib... or something."

"Or something? You don't think that might be an important detail?"

"It wasn't Zib, was it?" Azazel asked.

"Yea, that's it, Zib! And they called him something else too...Bander? Or band member? It was hard to hear because of the wind."

Lucifer and Azazel exchanged looks. Lucifer got up and began pacing. As he walked to the other side of the room he passed the mirror, something caught his eye. He stopped abruptly and turned to face the mirror, he stared over his shoulder at the name written in slime... his mind began to race! He felt his face go pale "No!" He said under his breath... "No, no, no... no way... they wouldn't!"

Lucifer spun around and pointing at Azazel he shouted, "GO! GO NOW! MEET ME IN ROME!" He turned to the screamer as Azazel left, "YOU! GO GET EVERY DEMON, EVERY GOBLIN, EVERY GHOST, EVERY

GATHERER AND ALL THE SCREAMERS YOU CAN FIND AND GET TO THE VATICAN! I'LL MEET YOU THERE, I WANT TWO HUNDRED THOUSAND MEN, GOOOO!!!

Lucifer sat down at his desk, head spinning, eyes wide. He went back to the mirror, he stood there looking at the name. He ran back to his desk and threw open the drawer looking for a pen. Another drawer, he ripped the next drawer out of the desk and threw it across the room.

"Paper!! ARRRGGG! A piece of frickin' paper!!" He screamed. Finding it, he sat down at what was left of his desk and began to write down all seven names. As he did, one of the keepers appeared at his door "WHAT!" He yelled at the door.

"This one wants to see you."

Lucifer looked up as the keeper ushered Imlack into the room.

CHAPTER 23
A Plane Full of Rabbis

As morning broke, the storm dissipated to a light wind. Amy woke first to the sound of Chewy in the kitchen, and she could smell ham and eggs cooking. This was the first night that she had had a peaceful sleep. Her eyes went to Johnathan, he was on the floor with a blanket over his head. She smiled and thought of the kiss under the tree in the rain and her heart fluttered a bit. She got up, and as she passed him she purposely kicked him in the back. He moaned and threw the blanket off his head.

"Sorry." She whispered as she hurried off to the bathroom to fix her face and hair before he could get a good look at her.

Johnathan sat up, his back ached from sleeping on the floor. He stood up and fell over. He looked around for Amy, he was excited to see her, and he hoped she would be excited too.

"Hello sunchine," Miguel said from the Kitchen.

"Where's Amy?" Johnathan asked.

"She cannot be seen in her current condition." Zib said.

"What's her current condition?" Johnathan said quizzically.

"Morning hair." Miguel said. "Jou two will have to put aside jor situation until we get home. There will be time for jor romance when we are safe, ok? But it does not mean that jou can't flirt a little." He winked at Johnathan.

Chewy came out of the kitchen with ham and scrambled eggs for everyone. They all gathered around the table, and Miguel blessed the food and said, "Eat this with my blessing."

As they passed around the food, Amy appeared from the bathroom. Johnathan stood up as she entered, as any gentleman would. They all welcomed her, but Johnathan was in awe. *Man, she is beautiful,* he thought. She smiled at him as she thanked Miguel for her seat.

"Listen," Zib started, "it's almost Hanukkah. There are going to be planes full of Rabbis headed for Jerusalem, they'll go in droves. If we can find a chartered flight full of Rabbis...I'm just sayin' how much safer do you want?"

Miguel looked at Leahcim and said, "How many stones do you have left?"

Leahcim pulled out his pouch and opened it, "Two I think," as he opened the pouch his face went blank, he looked up in a panic. "The book!"

"What's wrong?" Miguel said.

"The book is gone, it must have fallen out on the plane and I didn't see it!"

"And the stones?"

"I have them, but if they got the book..."

"Then they would know where we're going," Zib said.

"We better get to key west and find some Rabbis going home," Leahcim said.

Pedro came in from outside, he looked at Miguel and motioned to the sky and all around and shook his head no.

"What's he saying?" Amy asked.

"He says there are no demons anywhere."

"They know!" Leahcim said.

"We can take one of the shuttles from the hotel, we're only sixty miles away." Zib said, as he flashed his security badge. Within thirty minutes the seven where on their way to Key West airport. Amy and Johnathan were sitting together behind Miguel and Leahcim. As they traveled across the Keys, dodging fallen trees and debris from the hurricane, it seemed quiet, uneventful, almost eerie.

"If they know we're going to Jerusalem, aren't they already there waiting for us?" Johnathan asked.

Leahcim looked at Miguel.

"If they have the book, they know a lot more than that." Miguel replied. "There could be millions of demons descending on the Holy Land right now as we speak. Not that that's something new, but they will have a plan of some kind. We are going to have to be very careful and get there quickly, before they can set up."

Zib caught Miguel's eyes in the mirror and shook his head and smiled. They made good time to the airport, Zib parked the bus in the shuttle lot and went inside. Miguel, Pedro and Chewy were checking for flights ready to clear whatever flight they found.

Amy and Johnathan got out and stood beside the bus.

"Are you ok?" Johnathan asked her.

"Yes," she said as she looked at the ground. "Are you?...I'm sorry I called you a trailer turd," she said.

Johnathan laughed. "That was actually a really good one. I'm sorry I called you an idiot...all the time." Johnathan said sheepishly. "Is it true you killed all your other drivers?"

"NO!... Not all of them." She said quietly, then smiled.

As they were talking, an old man came around the side of the bus, he was dirty and had a hoodie pulled over his head. A long grey beard with a raspy voice said, "Change? Got any change?" He didn't look up.

"No, I'm really sorry, we don't." Johnathan said.

The man looked up at the two, his eyes were black!

"You have no idea how sorry you're going to be." He scrambled away. "See ya soon!" He yelled as he walked away.

Johnathan swallowed hard and looked at Amy, her face was flush. He moved her back onto the bus. He looked at Leahcim.

"We just saw a Nephilim."

"Where?"

"He's right there," Johnathan pointed out the window of the bus, but the man was gone.

"He was right there. He said we're gonna be sorry, and then he said, see ya soon!"

"They're watching us." Leahcim said dreadfully.

As Zib and Miguel walked through the airport Pedro tapped Miguel on the shoulder and pointed. They could see whisperers ducking behind walls and around corners, watching as they passed.

"I see." Miguel said. None of the whisperers did anything, they just watched. "I don't thin it's going to matter what plane we're on my friends."

"Well, let's travel with friends anyway." Zib said. The four returned to the bus.

"Ok, we leave in two hours. We found a plane full of Rabbis, we'll be in Jerusalem by tomorrow afternoon." Miguel said. He looked at Johnathan and smiled. "Jou can celebrate the Shabbat with jour family, my Jewish friend! See I told jou I would get jou home!"

Johnathan again shook his head and looked at Amy, "I'm not...," Amy just smiled.

As the seven waited they sat in the back of the bus talking. There was an air of uneasiness, they were restless, and wanted to get moving. Amy and Johnathan had their backs to the door of the bus as they talked.

Suddenly a hand covered Amy's mouth, and an arm went around her throat. Another one grabbed Johnathan, holding him with a knife at his throat. Pedro and Miguel jumped up, it was the man in the hoodie, standing behind the two demons that were holding Johnathan and Amy. The demon holding the knife to Johnathan's throat was Zuek. The man in the hood was standing with his head down, his hoodie covering most of his face. They all stood silent, waiting for what would happen next, Amy was making muffled crying noises, her eyes wide in fear.

Johnathan could smell Zuek's breath, he could feel the blade against his neck. The man in the hood started to speak, but then he started twitching and shaking, and then he shouted, "STOP MOVING!" He looked up from under his hood, his eyes were solid black.

"Who are you?" Miguel asked.

The hooded man still shaking, responded, "I am Azazel."

"What do you want?" Miguel asked politely.

"A bargain," Azazel responded.

"Bargain?"

"I'll offer safe passage through the gate in exchange for Abraham's Bosom. The old place in the pit, for me and fifty others, and we want bodies from the pit, of our choosing." The old man he possessed dropped to his knees and threw himself from side to side.

"STOP MOVING OLD MAN!" Azazel screamed. He stood back up.

"Lucifer will not agree to this." Miguel said.

"I have sent Lucifer to Rome, he doesn't know where you're going."

"If we don't agree?"

"Then you won't make it to the gate, and I'll kill these two, right here, right now!"

"What if we can't make that deal?" Zib asked.

"DON'T TEST ME ZIBRAEEL! YOU CAN'T WIN THE FIGHT THIS WILL START!"

"We've beat more than you before," Zib replied.

"You have no army with you Bangla! The five of you against my soldiers... It would give me great pleasure to kill you!" The old man's body turned and fought to leave the bus. Azazel slammed him into a row of seats, "Get up!"

He turned back to Zib and Miguel, "Take the deal! You're running out of time!"

Miguel looked at Zib and Leahcim, they nodded.

"Deal. Bring the bodies jou want to the gate. Once we have passed through, Jou can go to hell and live happily ever after, ok?" Miguel said with a smirk.

Azazel left the old man, and he slumped to the floor. Zuek gagged as he kissed Johnathan's cheek and threw up on his shoes as he released him. The other demon let go of Amy and followed the others out.

Johnathan grabbed Amy, "Are you ok?"

She nodded her head yes as her knees buckled under her, she fell into one of the seats.

"Did we just make a deal with the devil?' Johnathan asked.

"Of sorts," Leahcim said.

Leahcim looked at Miguel and Zib. "They're figuring this out." He said.

"One more day my friend, we have one more day." Miguel replied.

The plane was only about half full, the group took empty seats in the rear of the plane. Johnathan and Amy took the three seats in the last row. Miguel and Pedro sat in the seats in front of them, and Leahcim and Zib were in the row across the aisle. Chewy sat as close to the galley as he could, next to the window and buckled in his satchel next to him.

Johnathan looked out the window as the plane left the ground. Amy with her head on his shoulder watched as the plane veered off and out over the ocean. She wondered if they would ever see the United States again. They sat holding hands as the plane roared through the sky toward an unsure future.

As the sun set over the ocean below, they flew... safe for the first time in days or weeks. It had been so long since the car crash, so much had happened. Amy turned to Johnathan, and in a quiet voice she asked, "What's going to happen to us... I mean, where do you think we'll go?"

"Honestly...I just don't know," he replied. He looked at Amy, her eyes were full of tears.

"I've been so rotten my whole life, and I see that now. The horrible things I've done to so many people." She was sobbing now. "I know we're going somewhere tomorrow that holds us accountable, and I know I've just wasted my life and done so much damage to so many others... and I've just ignored God." She put her head back on his shoulder. "I just want Him to forgive me!" She sobbed.

"I know." Johnathan said. She looked at him with a hurt look. "No...I don't mean that I know you're rotten," he stammered, "I meant, I understand what you're saying. I've done some stuff I know was just...not good."

"You? Sweet, quiet Johnathan? I can't imagine you doing anything to ever offend anyone... besides me, but I deserved it."

"No...you have no idea." He shook his head.

"What?" She said.

"I've always believed in God... but when my parents died... I just couldn't even talk to Him anymore...," he paused for a long time. "I just knew He hated me... so I went off the deep end and did some terrible stuff ya know? I figured if He didn't want me, then I didn't want Him either. I started doing drugs and getting high all the time... and I dropped out of school."

Johnathan took a deep breath. "One night, I was really drunk, and I took my Dad's bible and went outside and covered it with gas and lit it up. I felt like another piece of me died when I did it." He was tearing up. "Anyway, after that I lost my job and couldn't pay my rent anymore, so I started stealing and doing whatever I could to stay alive. I stole an old man's wallet once... to buy booze. I think about that sometimes and wonder what if that was all he had in the world, ya know?" He looked at her and smiled sadly.

"And now I'm on my way to meet the man who wrote the book I burned, not to mention the yelling at the barn. Maybe He didn't hear me."

She wiped a tear off his cheek.

Johnathan clutched her hand tightly and said, "I hope He forgives us, and I hope you and I have some more time, together I mean." Miguel sitting in front of them was eavesdropping. He smiled and said under his breath, "Tetelestai."

CHAPTER 24
The Gate

The closer they got to Israel the more Amy and Johnathan wished they didn't have to be there. After all they had been through, the car crash, the demons, the gun fight, the dreams the sky diving this was the climatic end to either their lives or their eternity. They didn't know what to hope for, and they were scared to say the least. As the pilot announced their beginning descent Leahcim came over and sat next to Amy, he leaned over and asked, "How are you guy's doing?"

"Scared," Amy replied.

"Terrified," Johnathan added.

Leahcim reached in his pouch and took out the red stone, he handed it to Amy.

"This is the most important stone you'll ever hold, and you must not lose this stone. Without it the gateway won't open – and it must be in one of your hands, ok?"

"Yes...ok." Amy replied.

"It just has to cross the threshold of the gateway, ok?"

"Ok." Amy had not seen Leahcim be this serious before, it only worried her more.

Leahcim continued, "I don't have to be there, neither does Miguel, or Zib. As long as it's one of you, so if something happens just go for the gateway, ok? And stay together, ok? No matter what, it's important that you are together, ok?"

"Ok," she replied nervously.

Miguel had turned around in his seat, standing on his knees, peering over the back of the seat, as Pedro, Chewy and Zib came and stood next to them. "Jou two have been through a lot, I know this, and now our journey together is going to end soon. Jou both now believe, and this is a good thin, but it is just the beginning. Jou know a very wise man once said, 'Narrow is the gate, and difficult is the way, and few find it.' What this means is jor journey is just started, now today jou believe, that is the first step and it's good. From here jou need to trust in the one jou believe in, and remember He said that He will never leave jou or forsake jou. Jou must trust in Him now." Amy was crying as Johnathan held her hand tightly.

Zib looked at them and said, "When we get to Jerusalem, we're going to the temple mount, if we get separated just head for the Dome, you can't miss it. If we're not there for some reason just keep heading for the big gold dome. When you're at the site the gate should appear to you, just trust that God has this in His hands, this is your first day of faith, ok?"

"Ok," Johnathan said.

As the plane landed Johnathan and Amy's hearts were pounding. Every step they took as they walked down the aisle and moved through the airport. As they reached the taxi, and with every inch that they moved closer to the temple mount their hearts raced faster, Amy thought hers would explode.

As they drove to Jerusalem and entered the city, Johnathan began to see demons. They were everywhere... walking the streets, whisperers standing behind people, gatherers standing in alleyways, and as their cab passed them they began to follow the car. Coming out from every alley, bar, hotel, and market... they all just began to follow their car. Not rushing in to kill or capture but walking slowly behind the car... following.

It was getting late, the sun was beginning to set as they pulled in front of an old cemetery, near the Lions gate of the old temple.

"Is this it?" Amy asked, she could barely muster the words.

"We'll get out here and walk up." Leahcim said.

It was getting cold and the thought of walking through a cemetery made the whole thing seem worse. As they entered the grounds Chewy grabbed Amy and hugged her, he squeezed her tightly. As he let go he handed her a Twinkie, she smiled and kissed his cheek. Pedro gave her a hug and kissed her forehead. They moved off to stand guard at the entrance to the cemetery, they were all on guard, and they were all still tired from the long flight. Miguel moved ahead of the group and disappeared from Amy's sight.

Leahcim and Zib were just steps ahead of Amy and Johnathan, as they came around the last of the large tombstones they saw a group of about fifty men. They were just a few feet away from the wall of the temple mount and they were just standing there, watching them approach, Most were wearing dirty off-white clothes, stained with blood and dirt, and all of their eyes were as black as coal. None of them moved, they just stood and watched.

A cold chill ran up Johnathan's back. They were the fifty souls Azazel had taken from the pit that were now possessed by his soldiers.

One stepped forward, "I kept my word Zibraeel, now keep yours! "

Leahcim pointed to the wall, a small gate had appeared, the iron gates were rusted and the wood around them was old and dried by the years. The gates were set back a few inches from the threshold, the passageway was just large enough for two people, standing shoulder to shoulder, to pass through.

Leahcim motioned for Amy and Johnathan to move to the gate. Johnathan took Amy's hand and they moved around the group of demons slowly, Amy could hear them whispering as she passed. Suddenly they heard a whistle from below them. At the same time the ground began to shake, and they heard a rumble coming up from the bottom of the hill. They turned and saw hundreds and thousands of demons coming towards them.

The air filled with the screams of the demons running towards them. Lucifer was riding a black horse galloping towards Pedro. Hundreds of them pushed their way up the hill with intent.

Amy watched in horror as they reached Pedro and Chewy, they separated the two and thousands of them surrounded each man. She could see Pedro swinging a large branch, hitting demons, and splitting their heads open with every blow, she watched as the demons swarmed around him closing the circle tighter and tighter. She looked over to Chewy, he was fighting so hard, swinging his satchel violently. The mass of demons closed in on him quickly and engulfed him. She screamed as he disappeared into the swarm, swallowed by the sea of demons around him. Pedro was still fighting, he could see over the demons as he watched his faithful companion disappear into their midst, he screamed as he swung his branch but was overcome by their vast numbers and he also was overcome and disappeared into the swarm.

Lucifer appeared out of the drove, his horse dancing and rearing as he approached, he was carrying a sword dripping with blood.

Johnathan moved Amy behind him still holding her hand they were just a few feet from the gate...

Lucifer wiped the blood from his sword as he jumped from his horse and moved towards the group.

"I love the old language, don't you?" He said. "This day and age we've lost so much of the deeper meaning of words, they just aren't as full of impact as the old language was."

Leahcim started to move towards the gate.

"Leahcim, stop!" Lucifer demanded.

Leahcim kept moving.

"LEAHCIM, I SAID STOP!"

Leahcim took a few more steps.

"MICHAEL. STOP."

Leahcim stopped in his tracks and stood straight up, pushing his shoulders back, he was facing Johnathan and Amy, and suddenly his face changed. His whole appearance changed, the robe he had been wearing turned from a dingy brown to a snow colored white, his hair was now long and black, he had a slight beard. Amy and Johnathan watched in amazement as he transformed.

"Leahcim...Michael....Leahcim....Michael...," Lucifer started, "MICHAEL THE ARCHANGEL! Michael spelled backwards? Are you kidding me? That's the best heaven could do?!" He moved over to Michael, forced him to his knees, and took the pouch from his waist. He turned and looked at Zib.

"OH, AND ZIB...Really? ... Zib!? Bangla, Zibraeel...GABRIEL! Come on you guys!" He turned to the demons and Azazel and yelled, "DO I? DO I REALLY COME OFF AS THAT STUPID? You guys really thought that if you used the old language and spelled a few words backwards, I somehow wouldn't catch on!? Really?"

"OH, OH, OH, AND MY FAVORITE OF ALL...MIGUEL! Wait for it! Miguel Lesous Perez!" He looked at Azazel. "JESUS!... THE CHRIST HIMSELF!... THE SON OF GOD !... MEXICAN FIRST NAME, GREEK MIDDLE NAME, AND A JEWISH LAST NAME... BRILLIANT!" He turned back to Johnathan and Amy.

"Where is the Son of God anyway? He seems to have forsaken you guys," he leaned in towards them, "He gets that from his Dad." He walked swiftly towards Azazel.

"And as for you Az, you almost had me in Rome! But thanks to some who are still loyal to my cause, and still believe in me," he motioned for Imlack to come forward, "you were found out!"

He looked at the fifty demons, "Which one of you is Zuek?" None of them stepped forward. Azazel put his hand on the back of one of the demon's neck and thrust him forward. Lucifer walked over to him and thrust his sword into his stomach, as he stared into the demons eyes, the sword cut through the demon's spinal cord and he slumped to the ground paralyzed.

"Put him back in his hole." He motioned to two of the gatherers beside him, they picked up Zuek and dragged him away.

He turned back to Azazel. "Did you know it's almost impossible to kill a disembodied spirit? I mean how can you kill something, first of all that you can't see half the time, and secondly that's already dead?"

He was turning in circles, looking at all of them. He walked back over to Azazel.

"LOT! THAT'S HOW!" He turned to Gabriel, "I was there that day too. I watched what you two did in Sodom, but I especially watched you Gabriel. I saw you take a stone from your pouch and turn Lot's wife into a pillar of salt! That was cool! He took the last two stones from the pouch and threw the pouch at Michael.

Azazel started to move toward Lucifer. He began to speak but stopped, his legs were very heavy, he couldn't move, it was as if he were stuck in cement. He felt the sensation moving up his body, his eyes were wide, he looked franticly at the other demons. He tried to reach out for Lucifer, but as he did his eyes covered over with salt and he was frozen there, gazing at Lucifer arm stretched out.

"A PILLAR OF SALT! YEA BABY!" Lucifer howled. "This my friend was your biggest mistake." He said, as he turned to Michael, and held up the book.

"Ya know, I had the hardest time deciding what to do with all of you." He turned and motioned to Johnathan and Amy. "I mean technically... these two are mine. Undecideds should always be mine, but then when I discovered that you were with them, I thought to myself, well maybe this angel would be a nice prize to have. So, I'll let the two humans go, I mean hell is getting a little crowded anyway right?"

He turned back to Michael. "I had pretty much decided to kill you and just hope that this nightmare would end." As he was speaking he raised his arm, and a hundred archers stepped forward. "Then, thanks to my stony friend over there...," he gestured towards Azazel, "I figured out there were two of you here." He paused, "Alone, with no help."

He looked at Johnathan and Amy.

"TRAHERE!" He shouted. "I love the old language," he said smiling.

With that the archers drew their bows back, they cracked as they pulled them, the sound was like leather being stretched and pulled hard, multiplied by thousands.

"LUCIFER DON'T!" Michael shouted.

The archers were pointing at Amy and Johnathan. Johnathan moved in front of Amy again, she held his hand so tightly, her fingers were white, both barely breathing.

"I've decided that you two will stay here with me, and rather than give God any glory at all, I'll kill the humans. I mean that's what all this fuss is about right? So, I'll get the best of both worlds, excuse my pun, but I kill His treasure and I get mine!"

"DON'T DO THIS LUCIFER!"

"Or *what* Michael? I won't get into heaven? God will be mad?"

He looked Michael in the eyes and shouted, "IGNIS!" And he dropped his arm.

Johnathan watched as the arrows flew through the air, his eyes were wide as he watched them approach, everything seemingly moving in slow motion. He heard them as they were coming closer, they made a swooshing sound, he heard them crash against the wall behind them and he felt the splinters from the arrows shattering against the rock wall. Suddenly he was on his knees, he didn't remember ducking down, it was strange he thought, he couldn't hear anything anymore. He looked back at Amy, he could see she was screaming and holding his hand, but he couldn't hear her. He felt a warm and wet feeling, as he looked away from Amy, he looked at his chest, three of the arrows had found their mark. Two more were in his legs, he looked back at Amy as she faded from sight. He slumped at Amy's feet.

Amy was screaming, crying, "OH GOD, JOHNATHAN! NO!" She had to save him, she pulled on one of the arrows in Johnathan's chest, it wouldn't move. She tried another one, if she could just get them out she thought.

"JOHNATHAN!" She screamed, and she heard Lucifer yell...

"TRAHERE!"

The stone! She thought, *The stone! The gate!* She searched her pocket frantically, she found it, and she took Johnathan's hand and began to pull his lifeless body towards the gate.

Johnathan's hand in hers, the stone in the other she reached for the gate. He was too heavy, and she was too far away! She pulled at him as hard as she could, inching closer to the gate.

"IGNIS," She heard.

She stood straight up, as she did she heard the arrows crash against the rocks. The last arrow struck her hard in the middle of the chest, it took her breath away. The force of the arrow pushed her backwards... she fell holding Johnathan's hand, she couldn't breathe. She looked up at Michael, he tilted his head sideways and gave a slight smile and nodded his head. She reached out with her other hand as she fell over on her side, and she died before her hand hit the ground.

Her hand opened, and the stone rolled out and slowly tumbled across the threshold of the gate.

CHAPTER 25
The End...Well, Almost

Lucifer, Michael and Gabriel watched as the stone rolled over the old wood threshold. It bounced slightly and stopped at the iron gates. They all heard it coming, the sound of wind from behind the gate... it got louder and louder and suddenly the iron gates blew apart as the hurricane force wind ripped through the gates. It blew them apart and sent the pieces flying past Lucifer.

As the mighty wind hit him he stumbled backward losing his footing and it knocked him off his feet and rolled him down the hill. He only stopped when he hit a large headstone. The wind tore through the demons casting them aside like rag dolls, and it stopped when it came to Pedro's and Chewy's bodies. As quickly as the great wind had started, it stopped. Then from behind the gate, a very light, blue light came through the gate and moved slowly down the same path the wind had taken. The light engulfed Michael first, then moved slowly to Gabriel and moved on to Pedro and then Chewy.

As Lucifer picked himself up off the ground, he turned and looked to his army of demons, or rather where his army used to be. There was a sea of white horses with riders, swords drawn and on fire, the horses were pushing his demons down the hill. The riders held their swords in the air and he watched as his army began to scatter. They stumbled over each other as they retreated, disappearing into Jerusalem and the surrounding hills. He turned back and saw inside the light, there were four angels, they were carefully laying Amy on a thick white sheet. Four more appeared from within the light and gathered up Johnathan. Then they made their way down the hill, they walked slowly and stopped when they came to Pedro and Chewy. They never spoke, and without effort they picked up Chewy first, then Pedro. They took their lifeless bodies off the battlefield and carried them back to the gate and disappeared.

It was now just Lucifer, Michael and Gabriel. Michael got up from his knees and brushed off his robe, then he looked at Lucifer.

"Well...nice try." He shrugged his shoulders.

Lucifer stammered, "This... this isn't over!"

"Oh yea, it's over. We got what we came for." He motioned to where Amy and Johnathan had been laying.

Lucifer stepped forward and held up the book. "I have the book! And I have the two of you, and the stone!" He opened his hand and showed the last stone.

"There is no book Lucifer, there's never been a book! Gabe, did you ever have a book?"

"I never had a book." Gabriel said.

"I wish we would have had books, but no, no book Lucifer. There's only one book that ever came out of heaven and that ain't it!"

Lucifer turned and pointed to Azazel, "I turned him to salt! With the book and the stone!"

"Oh yea, thanks for that! We've been trying to get those guys for a long time! Good job! Well Gabe, should we go?"

"Yea, I've seen enough."

With that, Michael and Gabriel walked back into the light and disappeared into the gate.

CHAPTER 26
The Trial

Amy opened her eyes. It was so bright, she shaded her eyes with her hand. She could hear a distant voice, but it sounded so far away.

"Amy.... Amy...," the voice kept calling her name. "Amy look at me." The voice was closer and clearer now, it was familiar... it sounded like Leahcim.

She looked in the direction of the voice, it was Leahcim! She sat up excitedly, "Leahcim!" She shouted happily.

"Hello." He smiled.

Johnathan was standing next to Leahcim, smiling at her. Leahcim looked like Leahcim, just as he had for the last weeks of adventure.

"I don't understand," she said, as she examined her body.

"I'm the real Leahcim." He said as he began to explain, "Michael and I switched, sort of. I am your guardian, well almost... I stayed here and guided while he acted like me, so we could get you home safely. Michael is my trainer, has been for a long time, but after today I'm your official guardian!" He smiled.

"But the arrows... and Johnathan was dead!"

"It was all a fake, a ruse to keep Lucifer at bay."

"So, where are we? Are we dead now? I mean for real."

"Heaven and well...sort of. I mean we'll know for sure in a few minutes. We have to get moving, the trial is about to start again, we can't miss closing arguments."

"What trial?" Johnathan asked.

"Yours, that's why heaven was closed remember? This is about the two of you, this trial, these past few days... you died undecided remember?"

"Heaven was closed for our trial? But we would have never been in the accident and died in the first place if you hadn't gotten stuck!" Suddenly Johnathan understood.

"So we would believe." He said as he looked at Amy.

"There's nothing He won't do to get his children back." Leahcim said.

Johnathan took Amy's hand and helped her to her feet. "Are you ok?" He asked and kissed her.

"I think so...," She began to look around at her surroundings. "This place is beautiful!" She exclaimed breathlessly. "The air is so...clean! It feels so good here, LOOK!" She pointed to a lion, he was huge! Suddenly a child pounced on the lions neck from the grass, then two more piled on! The lion laid on his side and as the children continued to pile on top of him, they were all laughing and screaming with delight.

They walked, mouths open in awe of the sights and sounds. There were animals everywhere, every kind of animal, cats, dogs, elephants, giraffes... you name it... it was like a zoo with no fences.

The kids were running and playing with the animals, she saw the biggest bear she had ever seen, be tackled by a five-year-old boy dressed in a cowboy hat and chaps. She stopped and watched the two play as the bear hugged him and began licking the lad, the boy pushed away from the bear and stated in a very stern voice "I'n a cowboy an your apposed to be a mean ol gridly bear" He was pointing his little finger at the bear " NO LIKIN". It filled Amy's heart with Joy. The sky was filled with birds that sang continually, Amy could hear their songs, it was praise to God, beautiful sounds that she understood! The trees and plants were all perfectly groomed, not by men, they just grew that way.

As far as she could see there were rivers and creeks and huge fields of grass and mountains that reached the sky! She had a new understanding that she couldn't explain. It didn't need explaining, she just knew that this place was heaven and she really had no questions that needed answered. It was complete, with peace unlike anything else she had ever felt.

"Are there dinosaurs here?" Johnathan asked.

"Everything God has ever created is here." Leahcim answered.

They had reached a great building that seemed to reach way beyond the clouds. It sat in the middle of a grass field, surrounded by fountains and shrubs, with stone walkways that circled the great building. The doors to the building were at least twenty feet high and twenty feet wide. Great pieces of carved wood, they were open, and people were going in and out, all smiling and laughing, no one looked sad or worried. As they entered the great hall they passed a large curtain, it looked very old. It was blue and purple and scarlet, and it had two cherubs embroidered into the cloth, it was split down the middle as if it had been torn in two, with one Cherub on either side. As they passed between the two curtains Johnathan asked about them.

Leahcim replied, "That is the old veil, He likes to keep them here to remind us that anyone can come to Him now... to the throne room that is and talk with Him."

Johnathan realized that they were entering the throne room were God had wept, in the story Leahcim had told. They entered the main throne room, it was amazing. The room was circular, the bottom half of the walls were hand carved stone with beautiful images of trees and animals. The upper half of the walls were all wood, dark rich wood. Carved by hand was a continuous grape vine that circled the room, with its branches and leaves, and grape clusters growing all over the branches.

In the center of the room there was one table on the right, that had a sign that read <u>Defendant</u>. A few feet away was a second table with a sign that read <u>Accuser</u>. Each table had three chairs pulled up and neatly tucked underneath. In front of the tables was a large, curved wooden staircase that stretched from one side of the room to the other, and it led up to a huge throne that was made from what looked like roots from a massive tree, twisted, old wood. The seat, arms and back of the throne looked like one large mass of roots coming up from the floor. They continued upward to a single beam that rose above the throne and balanced on top of that beam was another beam of wood that spread across the top and led to two scales on either side of the beam. The scales were hung by three cords of gold rope, each strand was twisted together with three other strands of gold rope, which led down to the trays of fine pounded gold. The scales of justice. At the bottom of the staircase was a large desk built of the same roots as the throne. There was a small light shining from behind the desk, Amy could see someone sitting at the desk but couldn't make out his face.

Leahcim led Amy and Johnathan inside and seated them at the defense table.

"Do we have a lawyer? Johnathan asked.

"He's not here yet." Leahcim replied.

"What do you mean?"

"Don't worry," Leahcim winked and took his seat behind the two. The jury had already been seated, twelve very old looking men, white robes, all were looking down at their laps, hands covered by their sleeves. A very somber looking group of men.

Johnathan looked at them and worried. He reached over and took Amy's hand, she looked equally worried and smiled a half smile.

"ALL RISE, THE HONORABLE GOD ALMIGHTY, RULER OF HEAVEN AND EARTH PRESIDING."

Everyone stood and then went to their knees and bowed their heads before the throne, as His presence entered the room. Johnathan and Amy did not look up, the presence was thick with awe and a sense of wonder.

"Be seated."

Amy and Johnathan stood up and took their seats, they both looked up at the throne. There was a cloud surrounding the throne from the arms up. They couldn't see God's face only his feet, legs and arms were visible. He wore a white robe and sandals that tied with straps half way up his calf. His presence took Amy and Johnathan's breath away. They sat speechless.

It was quiet in the courtroom, suddenly the jury erupted in cheers and yelling, Amy jumped in surprise. She looked around the room, they had all jumped to their feet and were yelling and high fiving each other.

"ORDER! ORDER!" He yelled from the throne.

They had been watching a football game with iPods! That's why their heads were down looking at their hands and looking so somber!

"Bailiff take those." A collective "AWWW" came from the jury box.

A man emerged from behind the desk, and as he came out of the shadows Amy saw him,

"CHEWY!" she shouted.

Chewy looked at her and smiled and gave a small wave, as he approached the jury box with a small basket. He had a half unwrapped, half eaten beef stick in his mouth. He gathered all the devices from the jurors and handed them to the throne as he turned to return to his seat at the desk.

"Chewy," Chewy stopped and took another bite.

"Chewy," the voice said again.

Chewy turned and returned to the throne and handed over his beef stick, with his head down he went back to his desk.

"Bronco's 21-7," from the throne.

Another collective "AHH!" from the jury box.

"Alright, alright, bring in the accuser, let's let him finish his closing arguments and be done with this."

With that there was a collective hiss from the onlookers as Lucifer entered the room. Amy and Johnathan watched as Lucifer entered. He was dressed in a solid black silk suit, red tie, red socks and black leather shoes. His hair was slicked back and pulled into a ponytail. He took his place at the accuser's table, opened his hands and said, "Ok then...," He moved from behind the table and approached the jury box. "This, as you've all seen, is at best a farce, a pack of lies put on by heaven to save these two from, what surely should be, their final destiny." He paused for effect. "The PIT." He continued, "As you have all witnessed, these two have spent their whole lives either denying or ignoring the call that heaven has put out for them. And this one," he pointed to Johnathan, "has been drinking, stealing, and lying his way through life! She's no better, how many lives, as she herself has fully admitted, how many lives did she trash to get what she wanted? How many? I submit that these souls are mine, they never would have asked for forgiveness if heaven hadn't intervened!" His voice was reaching a high pitch as he began

yelling, "THIS IS ALL A BIG FAT HAIRBALL, SPIT UP BY MIGUEL AND HIS CRONIES, TO CHEAT ME OUT OF MY SOULS! YOU MUST DO WHAT IS RIGHT, YOU MUST GIVE ME WHAT IS MINE!"

He began pointing at everyone in the room.

"YOU LIED, YOU LIED, HE LIED, I'M ENTITLED TO THESE SOULS!!"

"Are you done Lucifer?" From the throne.

"YES, I'M DONE! I'M DONE WITH THIS KANGAROO COURT AND ALL THE LIES! YOU'RE SUPPOSED TO BE ALL GOOD AND ALL PERFECT, BUT YOU DO ANYTHING YOU WANT TO SAVE THESE PIGS!"

He was really worked up now.

"SIT!" Said the voice from the throne. With that, Lucifer stomped to his chair and flopped down like an insolent child.

"DEFENSE." God said.

With that everyone in the room stood to their feet as the doors to the court opened. Amy could just see the top of the heads of two men as they entered the room. And then, from the back of the room to the front, as the men passed, everyone got on their knees. As they reached the front tables, Lucifer stood shaking, fighting the urge to kneel...

then as if someone had pushed him down, he went to his knees, grinding his teeth as he did.

Amy and Johnathan were on their knees also and looked up. It was Pedro! He was dressed in a white flowing robe, girded with a leather sash that held a mighty sword. His hand on his sword, he escorted the defense attorney to stand in front the throne. Amy and Johnathan had yet to see his face, but from the back they could see he had shoulder length black hair, his robe was also as white as snow, with sandals on his feet. Their hearts were pounding, the anticipation was intense... they could hardly stand the suspense of his opening words. The room was completely silent with the exception of Lucifer, fighting to remain on his knees.

Amy's memory suddenly flashed back to Leahcim's story of 'just four words...This one is mine'... "Oh God," she said out loud.

"Yes?" said the voice from the throne, and everyone in the room turned and looked at her.

"Oh...no...I'm sorry...I was just...nothing." Amy stammered.

"YOU HAVE CLOSING STATEMENTS?" from the throne.

Everyone knew this was the moment, the defense would use four words or so, sometimes more but the usual was four. It determined the eternal fate of the one on trial. Heaven had spent this person's life trying to influence their decision, trying to get them to come home, to turn to God and away from their dark ways.

Johnathan flashed back to the conversation he had had in the stall, yelling at God, the remorse he'd had for the life he had led. He hung his head and hoped God had heard his cries. It all came down to this, the one decision in a lifetime of decisions, the one to turn to God. Had they? Neither were really sure if God had heard them, and if He did, was it really enough to save them? What if it weren't true and you had to lead the perfect life!? What if all these people in heaven were just the best of the best? Oh Amy wished she had looked at them closer to see if they were shiny and crispy clean! Did she look like them? Oh no she couldn't remember! Then she remembered the junkie in the building, and the words Leahcim had said. Johnathan was remembering the words too. Leahcim had told them about heaven... "if everyone had to be perfect then heaven would be empty."

All these memories came flooding back to them, all the stories he had told, in a moment they would know if they were true...

The defense attorney turned and faced Amy and Johnathan.

It was Miguel !

Standing there in a robe so white it almost blinded them. He turned to Johnathan and Amy and stretched out his arms and said, "THESE TWO ARE MINE!"

"CASE DISMISSED!" Came the booming voice from the throne.

The courtroom erupted in cheers and smiles, the jurors all stood and high fived each other again and smiled at them as they filed out.

Lucifer rolled his eyes and got off his knees and quickly left the room.

Amy collapsed to her knees. Johnathan reached over and picked her up and hugged and kissed her. She was of course crying. He smiled at her and they both turned to Miguel.

He smiled and said in very clear English, "Yes, of course I heard you! Even though jour English is not so good my friend!" He was looking at Johnathan grinning. He turned and holding Amy by the shoulders, he smiled and said, "Now my child, your journey begins. I love you and I will never leave you. "you just have to call on me, I will walk with you all the days of your life, abide in me and I will abide in you" He gently kissed her forehead and put his hand on Johnathan's shoulder, giving a gentle squeeze. Then he turned and walked up the gnarled steps and disappeared into the cloud around the throne.

They stood there in awe. The weight of the world had just been lifted from them. They turned to Leahcim.

"What do we do now, I mean what happens now?" Amy asked.

Leahcim began to speak, but he was moving away from them. Something was pulling them backward toward the door of the throne room, his voice was being drowned out, they could see he was talking but they couldn't hear what he was saying. He was moving farther and farther away...he was fading! Amy looked at Chewy he smiled and waved at her, but he was fading away too...

CHAPTER 27
THE END

The nurse yelled across the room.

"We've got flight for life inbound with two onboard! Rollover accident, unrestrained, one male approximately twenty-five to thirty years old, head trauma, multiple lacerations and currently unconscious. Second victim a female approximately the same age, also unconscious, suffered suffocation, revived onsite. Get this, she was found face down in cow manure! Two minutes people! Let's go!"

Two stretchers burst through the doors of the emergency room, medics and nurses were working frantically on both patients.

As they worked on Johnathan he began to fight the doctors and nurses, they had a mask over his face and were working feverishly to stop the bleeding that seemed to be coming from everywhere. He kept grabbing at his oxygen mask and trying to pull it off.

"Calm down." The nurse kept saying, he kept struggling.

"Let's sedate him."

As the nurse approached him with the needle he reached up and ripped the mask from his face and screamed, "AMY!"

He drifted off into unconsciousness again, as the sedation took quick effect.

Amy was in the next room, they were clearing her airway, frantically working to get her breathing on her own. She was drifting in and out, she looked up and saw the male nurse reach across her as he checked her respirator. She saw on his forearm tattooed in a circle faith=hope=faith=hope= . She looked at him... it was the junkie from the abandoned building. A faint smile came across her lips as she slipped back into unconsciousness.

Leahcim stood at the foot of Johnathan's hospital bed. As his official guardian angel, he felt very compelled to stand guard over his new ward. As he stood there pondering the events of the last few weeks, his thoughts were broken up by a cold presence that filled the room.

"Let's go in," Lucifer whispered into Leahcim's ear.

His voice startled Leahcim. Lucifer was standing next to Leahcim, leaning into his shoulder and in a whispered, almost muffled voice he said, "Have you ever been inside the mind of someone in a coma?" Leahcim could feel the anger rising inside himself at the sound of Lucifer's voice.

"It's wonderful in there... a virtual blank canvassss." His small black forked tongue tickled the inside of Leahcims ear as he hissed the word.

"This is over Lucifer, they're saved!" Leahcim insisted.

Lucifer stepped around in front of Leahcim, keeping his hand on Leahcim's shoulder and looking into his eyes said, "What... are you new? It's never over white one, I'm just getting started!"

With that, Lucifer disappeared and entered Johnathan's mind, leaving Leahcim standing alone. Shaking from the exchange, Leahcim looked up toward heaven and said "Father?"

And then he followed Lucifer into Johnathan's mind.

Endnote

I hope you enjoyed the story. I would like to say that this story is not about Johnathan and Amy. This story is about YOU, the one reading this right now at this very moment. His love for you, that's what this story is about. No matter where you live, your color, age, gender matters not to Him. He wants your heart, He wants His child, He wants YOU. May the Lord bless you and keep you; May the Lord make his face to shine upon you and be gracious to you, May the Lord turn his face towards you and give you peace. [1]

You can reach me directly at ted-fulton@comcast.net

---

[1] Numbers 6:22-27

BIBLIOGRAPHY

New Living Translation Bible
NIV Bible
New American standard Bible
The Message Bible

13604206R00124

Made in the USA
San Bernardino, CA
14 December 2018